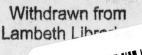

THE HELMET OF HORROR

VICTOR PELEVIN has established a reputation as
one of the most interesting of the younger genera-
tion of Russian writers. He has degrees from
Moscow's Gorky Institute of Literature and has
written for the *New York Times Magazine*, *Granta* and
Open City. He was selected by the *New Yorker* as one
of the 'Best European Writers Under 35' and by the
Observer as one of the '21 Writers for the 21st
Century'. His novel, *Numbers*, won the Grigoriev
Prize from the Russian Academy of Critics 2004..

ANDREW BROMFIELD is a regular translator from
the Russian, and has translated works by Boris
Akunin, Vladimir Voinovich and Irina Denezhkina,
as well as other titles by Victor Pelevin.

Also by Victor Pelevin

Novels

Short Stories

THE HELMET OF HORROR

The Myth of Theseus and the Minotaur

Victor Pelevin

Translated from the Russian by
Andrew Bromfield

CANONGATE
Edinburgh · London

First published in Great Britain in 2006 by
Canongate Books Ltd, 14 High Street,
Edinburgh, EH1 1TE

This edition published in 2007

British Library Cataloguing-in-Publication Data
A catalogue record for this book is available
on request from the British Library

978 1 84195 889 7 (13-digit ISBN)
1 84195 889 1 (10-digit ISBN)

Designed by Pentagram
Typeset in Van Dijck MT Regular bv
Palimpsest Book Production Limited

Printed and bound by Clays Ltd, St Ives plc

www.canongate.tv

Myths are universal and timeless stories that reflect and shape our lives — they explore our desires, our fears, our longings, and provide narratives that remind us what it means to be human. *The Myths* series brings together some of the world's finest writers, each of whom has retold a myth in a contemporary and memorable way. Authors in the series include: Chinua Achebe, Margaret Atwood, Karen Armstrong, AS Byatt, David Grossman, Milton Hatoum, Natsuo Kirino, Alexander McCall Smith, Tomàs Eloy Martínez, Victor Pelevin, Ali Smith, Donna Tartt, Su Tong, Dubravka Ugresic, Salley Vickers and Jeanette Winterson.

Mythcellaneous

'No one realised that the book and the labyrinth were
one and the same . . .'

Borges, *The Garden of Forking Paths*

According to one definition, a myth is a traditional
story, usually explaining some natural or social
phenomenon. According to another, it is a widely
held but false belief or idea. This duality of meaning is revealing. It shows that we naturally consider
stories and explanations that come from the past to
be untrue – or at least we treat them with suspicion.
This attitude, apart from creating new jobs in the
field of intellectual journalism, gives some additional
meaning to our life. The past is a quagmire of
mistakes; we are here to find the truth. We know
better.

The road away from myth is called 'progress'. It
is not just scientific, technical or political evolution.

Progress has a spiritual constituent beautifully expressed by F. Scott Fitzgerald in *The Great Gatsby*:

> [a belief] in the green light, the orgastic future that year by year recedes before us. It eluded us then, but that's no matter – tomorrow we will run faster, stretch our arms further . . . And one fine morning –
>
> So we beat on, boats against the current, borne back ceaselessly into the past.

In other words, progress is a propulsion technique where we have to constantly push ourselves away from the point we occupied a moment ago. However, this doesn't mean that we live without myths now. It only means that we live with instant myths of soap-bubble content. They are so unreal you can't even call them lies. Anything can become our mythology for fifteen minutes, even *Mythbusters* programme on the Discovery channel.

The foundation of this mind-set on progress is not faith, as happens with traditional cults, but the absence of it. However, the funny thing is that the concept of progress has been around for so long that now it has all the qualities of a myth. It is a traditional story that pretends to explain all natural and social phenomena. It is also a belief that is widespread and false.

Progress has brought us into these variously shaped and sized cubicles with glowing screens. But if we start to analyse this high-end glow in terms of content and structure, we will sooner or later recognise the starting point of the journey – the original myth. It might have acquired a new form, but it hasn't changed in essence. We can argue about whether we were ceaselessly borne back into the past or relentlessly pushed forward into the future, but in fact we never moved anywhere at all.

And even this recognition is a traditional story now. A long time ago Jorge Luis Borges wrote that there are only four stories that are told and re-told: the siege of the city, the return home, the quest, and the (self-) sacrifice of God. It is notable that the same story could be placed into different categories by different viewers: what is a quest/return home for Theseus is a brutal God's sacrifice for Minotaur.

Maybe there are more than just 'four cycles', as Borges called them, but their number is definitely finite and they are all known. We will invent nothing new. Why?

This is where we come to the third possible definition of a myth. If a mind is like a computer, perhaps myths are its shell programs: sets of rules that we follow in our world processing, mental matrices we project onto complex events to endow them with meaning. People who work in computer programming say that to write code you have to be young. It seems that the same rule applies to the cultural code. Our programs were written when the human race was young — at a stage so remote and obscure that we don't understand the programming language any more. Or, even worse, we understand it in so many different ways and on so many levels that the question 'what does it mean?' simply loses sense.

Why does the Minotaur have a bull's head? What does he think and how? Is his mind a function of his body or is his body an image in his mind? Is Theseus inside the Labyrinth? Or is the Labyrinth inside Theseus? Both? Neither?

Each answer means that you turn down a different corridor. There were many people who claimed they knew the truth. But so far nobody has returned from the Labyrinth. Have a nice walk. And if you happen to meet the Minotaur, never say 'MOOO'. It is considered highly offensive.

Started by ARIADNE at xxx p.m. xxx xxx BC GMT

I shall construct a labyrinth in which I can lose myself, together with anyone who tries to find me — who said this and about what?

:-)

Organizm(-:
What's going on? Is there anyone there . . . ?

Romeo-y-Cohiba
I'm here.

Organizm(-:
So what's going on round here?

Romeo-y-Cohiba
Your guess is as good as mine.

Organizm(-:
Ariadne, are you there?

Romeo-y-Cohiba
Who's she?

Organizm(-:
She started this thread. Seems this isn't the Internet, just looks like it. You can't link to anywhere else from here.

Romeo-y-Cohiba
xxx

Organizm(-:
Hello! If anyone can read this, please answer.

Nutscracker
I can read it.

Organizm(-:
Who posted the first message?

Nutscracker
It's been up on the board a long time.

Romeo-y-Cohiba
How can you tell? There's no date on it.

Nutscracker
I saw it three hours ago.

Organizm(-:
Attention, roll-call. There's just Nutcracker, Romeo
and me here, is that right?

Romeo-y-Cohiba
That's right.

Nutscracker
At least, we're the only ones who want to join in.

Romeo-y-Cohiba
Right, so there are three of us here.

Nutscracker
But where is here exactly?

Organizm(-:
How do you mean?

Nutscracker
Quite literally. Can you describe where you are now? What is it — a room, a hall, a house? A hole in someone's xxx?

Romeo-y-Cohiba
Well I'm in a room, anyway. Or a cell, I can't tell which is more correct. Not very big. Green walls, white ceiling lamp. A bed by one wall and by the opposite wall a desk with the keyboard I'm typing on right now. The keyboard is attached rigidly to the desk. Above the desk there's an LCD screen set in the wall behind thick glass. That's where all these letters appear. It's impossible to break, I tried already. The room has two doors, one made of strange, blackish-green metal. It's locked. There's a raised section in the middle of it. The other door's

made of wood, painted white, and it leads into a bathroom. It's open.

Organizm(-:
I've got the same as Romeo. A locked metal door with some kind of relief design on it. A hotel-style bathroom with soap, shower gel and shampoo on the shelf under the mirror. Everything in packaging marked with a strange symbol — something like a little cogwheel. So where are you, Nutcracker?

Nutscracker
In the same kind of room. I think the door's made of cast bronze. But Organism, the symbol on the soap looks more like a star than a cogwheel. In fact it looks like the symbol they use in books for a footnote. It's even on the loo paper, every sheet.

Romeo-y-Cohiba
So we're all in the same hotel. Let's try knocking on the walls. Can you hear anything?

Organizm(-:
No.

Nutscracker
Me neither.

Organizm(-:
I'll try knocking on the door, listen.

Romeo-y-Cohiba
I can't hear a thing.

Organizm(-:
So how did we get here?

Romeo-y-Cohiba
Personally speaking, I haven't got the slightest idea. How about you, Organism?

Organizm(-:
I just woke up here wearing this pooftah's housecoat with nothing underneath it.

Nutscracker

It's not a housecoat. It's a *chiton* – the kind of tunic the ancient Greeks used to wear, so I won't take issue with your opinion of it. I don't think they wore any underclothes either.

Romeo-y-Cohiba

It's a good job it's warm in here then.

Organizm(-:

So, maybe you remember how you got here, Nutscracker?

Nutscracker

No, I don't.

Romeo-y-Cohiba

Why have you two got such odd names – Organizm, Nutscracker?

Nutscracker

Well, why have you got such an odd name, Romeo? Is your *cohiba* really such a whopper?

Romeo-y-Cohiba
I suppose that depends whose you compare it with.
And anyway, it wasn't me who invented the name. It
just appears on the screen when I send a message.
I'm not Romeo, I'm xxx. A professional xxx, if
anyone's interested.

Organizm(-:
Porn business? Socially significant work. You and I
are almost colleagues, Romeo – I'm a xxx. I used to
work at xxx.com, so I'm temporarily out of a job.
But there's not much danger of that for you.

Romeo-y-Cohiba
How did the porn business get mixed up in all this?
And what are all these x's?

Nutscracker
That's not the first time they've appeared. It's the
censor. Someone's monitoring our conversation.
And he doesn't like it when we try to exchange
information about who we really are. Or start
swearing.

Romeo-y-Cohiba

Hey, you, whoever you are! I demand that you allow me to contact my family immediately! And the xxx embassy!

Nutscracker

What makes you think there's a xxx embassy here?

Romeo-y-Cohiba

There's a xxx embassy everywhere.

Nutscracker

Are you sure? What if we're in xxx?

Organizm(-:

Apparently you guys can understand each other without words. But I don't understand what the xxx embassy is, and where xxx is, if there's no xxx embassy there. And what the xxx you want it for anyway.

Monstradamus

Hi there, is it okay if I join in your discussion?

Organizm(-:
Who are you, Monstradamus?

Monstradamus
xxx. I live in xxx and I'm a xxx.

Romeo-y-Cohiba
Perhaps you ought to try something a bit more original?

Monstradamus
I've read all the messages on this thread. I'm in the same situation, the same room, the same fancy get-up. And I don't remember how I got here, either.

Nutscracker
So now we are four. That's nice.

Organizm(-:
What's so nice about it?

Nutscracker
Maybe more will turn up soon. The more heads we have,

the better our chances of coming up with something.

Organizm(-:
And what if we've simply died?

Nutscracker
Don't panic! Dead people don't hang around in chat rooms.

Organizm(-:
We don't know that for a fact. Maybe that's all they can do.

Romeo-y-Cohiba
If this is the afterlife, then I for one am disappointed.

Nutscracker
Let's discuss the situation. I suggest we don't take Organism's hypothesis about the afterlife into consideration.

Organizm(-:
Then maybe it's a dream?

Romeo-y-Cohiba
Pinch yourself. Maybe you'll wake up. I tried already, it didn't work.

Nutscracker
Right, so everybody has a bronze door. Let's try figuring out the design on that door. It's a figure like a rectangle with the upper and lower edges bent inwards and the sides bent outwards.

Organizm(-:
It looks like a bat. Or the Batman symbol.

Romeo-y-Cohiba
I reckon it's a double-headed axe.

Organizm(-:
Maybe it's just decoration, without any meaning. But Romeo saying it looks like an axe has made me think so too. The fascists used to have axes like that — or was it the ancient Romans?

Monstradamus
If it is an axe, it's much older than Rome. They used
to have axes like that in Crete and ancient Egypt.

Organizm(-:
Are you a historian then, Monstradamus?

Monstradamus
No. I'm a xxx.

Organizm(-:
Hey, that's right. I forgot.

Ariadne
Hi. I'm glad I'm not the only one here.

Organizm(-:
Hi there, darling.

Romeo-y-Cohiba
Where there are boys, there have to be girls. Some
funny rainbow-coloured patches of light just
appeared on my walls.

Monstradamus

That's odd, I had them too. Or maybe I imagined it.

Nutscracker

Ariadne? Did you start this thread?

Ariadne

Yes. But no one answered, and I fell asleep.

Monstradamus

So why did you write that phrase about the labyrinth?

Ariadne

I was trying to remember where it came from, but I couldn't. I had the feeling it was very important.

Monstradamus

Who are you and how did you get here?

Ariadne

I'm in exactly the same situation as you.

Organizm(-:
In that case, we know all about you already. Your real name's xxx, you're xxx years old and you come from xxx.

Ariadne
I know what's going on here.

Nutscracker
How?

Ariadne
I saw it all in a dream.

Romeo-y-Cohiba
I don't think I'd exactly regard that as *bona fide* information.

Monstradamus
I wouldn't mind hearing about it, though. Tell us about it.

Ariadne

I saw this old city. I mean, really ancient. The kind they must have built thousands and thousands of years ago. It was really beautiful there. Roads paved with big, flat stones, stone walls covered with living curtains of some climbing plant with pale-pink flowers. The doors and windows of all the houses were locked, but all the time I had the feeling I was being watched by someone. I wandered round the streets for ages, but I didn't meet anyone. And then on the cross-roads up ahead of me I kept catching sight of a dwarf dressed in grey rags and a strange hat with a wide brim and a round crown. Every time I spotted him, he instantly darted round a corner, as though he could feel my gaze on his back. It happened lots of times, over and over again. Soon I realised he wasn't hiding from me, it was just that the rhythm of his movement was linked with the rhythm of mine so I couldn't see him for more than those few seconds. Only don't ask me how I realised it, in a dream everything has its own logic. I began trying to adjust to the rhythm, trying to get a better look at the dwarf. By choosing broad, straight streets, I could keep him in my field of vision for longer. But most of the streets were narrow and crooked – the way they linked up made a genuine labyrinth. I realised there were actually two dwarves, but it was easy to confuse the second one with the first. He was dressed in exactly the same way, in some old rags, only the brim of his hat was bent up on one side. Gradually I became certain there was someone else with them as well, but no matter how hard I tried, I couldn't see the third person. Sometimes I could just catch a glimpse of the edge of his dark cloak from round a corner. I guessed I needed to find the way to the main street – it would be long and wide and I would be able to see all of them . . .

Romeo-y-Cohiba
What's the point of us listening to all this?

Monstradamus
Please, don't interrupt. What happened after that, Ariadne?

Ariadne
After that I made my way to the main street. There

was a long line of palm trees in tubs along the middle
of it. I remember that what was most astonishing
was that there were yellow leaves everywhere, it was
autumn, and then here were these palm trees.

Nutscracker
You started off with pink flowers. Now suddenly it's
autumn, with yellow leaves.

Ariadne
Yes, autumn set in while I was following the dwarf.
I thought he must have done that on purpose to spoil
my mood and prevent me catching up with him.
There was no one in the main street. I came to a
large square with a fountain with bronze statues
standing in it. From their style I thought they must
be just as ancient as the city, but their subjects were
more like something from a Japanese cartoon film —
naked teenagers being strangled by tentacles twined
around their bodies. Or snakes . . .

Nutscracker
What have Japanese cartoons got to do with anything?

IsoldA

She's talking about *mangas*, young girls who are raped by demons with their tentacles. It's a persistent theme in Japanese virtual porn.

Monstradamus

It's an expression of the repressed subconscious frustration resulting from defeat in the Second World War. The schoolgirl raped in these cartoons symbolises the Japanese national spirit, and the monster that sprouts these multiple phallic tentacles represents the modern western-style corporate economy.

Nutscracker

Or maybe they're just octopuses?

Monstradamus

Octopuses? How original. I'd never have thought of that.

Organizm(-:

Hey, who is this Isolde? Someone new?

IsoldA
Yes.

Romeo-y-Cohiba
Welcome to our little world, Isolde. We're very pleased to meet you.

IsoldA
Thank you, Romeo.

Organizm(-:
Are you pretty?

Romeo-y-Cohiba
Get a grip, Organism.

Nutscracker
Isolde, can you add anything to the sum of our experience?

IsoldA
No.

Monstradamus

Then, if no one has any objections, Ariadne can continue.

Ariadne

I realised I had to go over to the fountain and then I would see both dwarves. Only don't ask me how I realised it; it was suddenly clear, that's all. When I reached the fountain I turned my back to it and leaned against the wall. Opposite me there was a building with a colonnade – a massive, depressing building with ugly superstructures on the roof. It occurred to me somehow that a long time ago it had been burnt down, and nothing was left but the stone skeleton, and since then a lot of attempts had been made to repair it and restore it to life. But you could still see the traces of the catastrophe through the restoration work and the paint, and you could tell the building was dead and empty . . .

Romeo-y-Cohiba

I'd say we need an entire committee of psychiatrists for this spiel. Or we could ask Monstradamus, he's got a good handle on this stuff. What was that phrase he used – corporate frustration?

Monstradamus
Romeo, please, be patient just a moment longer.

Ariadne
Suddenly I noticed one of the dwarves standing beside me – the one with the side of his hat bent up. I didn't see how he got there. He was really close to me, but I couldn't see his face under the hat. I remember he was wearing medieval-style pointed shoes in red and white stripes. He began speaking without raising his head, and what he said was very strange. He said the master he served was the creator of everything I saw around me, and a great many other things too. The way I understood it, this master of his was not a man. Or not just a man. His name was Asterisk . . .

Monstradamus
Are you sure you heard correctly?

Ariadne

I think so. The way the dwarf explained it, Asterisk is some boundlessly and infinitely powerful being. I asked whether he didn't mean God, and he said that God was merely Asterisk's errand boy. I asked how that was possible. The dwarf told me not even to try to understand. He said it was a great mystery, and repeated this several times. I asked him what was the correct name to use for someone who is mightier than God. Any name you like, the dwarf replied – the word 'Asterisk', or any other that can be spoken – they're no more than loose dust covers, they make no difference at all. That was what he said, honestly . . .

Romeo-y-Cohiba

What absolute gibberish.

Ariadne

The way I understood it, Asterisk is angry with people because at some time in the past they killed him. Or because they will kill him at some time in the future – the dwarf expressed himself in such a complicated manner, you could take his meaning any way at all. Since that time – or until that time – people have to pay tribute to Asterisk by sending him people to join in his games and die in his arena. Like us, for instance . . .

Nutscracker
Well, there you go then.

Ariadne
But the dwarf said there was no need to be upset, because the people Asterisk sacrifices to himself have already been born, and dying in the arena is the common fate that nobody escapes. I tried to ask in that case what was the point of the sacrificial tribute, but the dwarf began getting nervous and said, 'Look, he's coming, now you can see him for yourself.' I looked up. Two figures had appeared in front of the burnt-out building. Striding along solemnly in front was a dwarf holding a flag with the Merrill Lynch symbol on it – you remember it, they have that jolly little bull – and the inscription 'Be Bullish!' But I didn't feel like laughing at all, the

figure following it looked so terrifying. I don't even know what to call him. He wasn't like a man. He was absolutely massive, and I thought for a moment he was a monstrously overgrown mushroom with a big cap of blackish-green metal. Then I took a closer look at him. He was wearing a long loose robe that reached right down to the ground, dark-coloured and not particularly clean either, but not the same kind of tattered rags as the dwarves. And on his head he had a bronze helmet, like a gladiator's mask – a head-piece with a wide brim and a plate with holes in it where the face would be. There were two horns on the helmet . . . .

Monstradamus
Like a bull's horns?

Ariadne
They were much more massive and they didn't stick out to the sides, they ran backwards, merging into the helmet to form a single block. If I could compare them with anything, they looked a lot like the silencers of a bronze motorbike, curving along the rim of the

headpiece with the round crown. There were lots of little rods and tubes on the helmet as well, all made of bronze, and they linked all its different parts together, so the whole thing looked a bit like an antique rocket engine.

Nutscracker
Did he say anything?

Ariadne
No, I didn't see him for very long. I only had just enough time to think the two dwarves were dressed so strangely because they were trying to look like him. Beside him they looked absolutely tiny. And there seemed to be something wistful or sad and lonely about him, like someone who'd been banished by the emperor. Or just the opposite, as though he was an emperor who had been left all alone because he had banished everyone else.

Monstradamus
Is that how the dream ended?

Ariadne

I didn't see Asterisk again. Suddenly the dwarf and I were somewhere else, on one of the little streets, facing an old wooden door with a handle in the form of a ring set through the head of a bull. The dwarf knocked on the door with the ring and it opened. Inside there was a small room. From where we were standing all we could see was a bed with a man sleeping on it, a tall man with a moustache and a mole beside his nose. The dwarf muttered that we were in the wrong place, led me to a different door and opened it in the same way. The room behind it looked the same, but it was empty. The dwarf raised his finger and asked, 'I shall construct a labyrinth in which I can lose myself, together with anyone who tries to find me – who said this and about what?' I started thinking about it – in the dream I almost knew the answer. Then suddenly he pushed me inside and slammed the door shut.

Monstradamus

What happened after that?

Ariadne

The push woke me up and I found myself in the room I am in now. Then I sat down at the desk with the screen and typed in that question. I was afraid I might forget it. But I can still hear it in my head now.

Monstradamus

Is it the same room as you entered in the dream?

Ariadne

It's hard to say. It's just as small.

Romeo-y-Cohiba

And who was the man with the mole beside his nose?

Ariadne

I don't know. I'd never seen him before.

Romeo-y-Cohiba

Can you describe him in more detail? Exactly where was this mole of his?

Ariadne
Between the side of the nostril and the cheek. He had a horseshoe moustache too. And he was absolutely bald. Big. I definitely remember that his arm was lying on the pillow and it had a tattoo on it, an anchor with a dollar sign twisted round it. I though it might be a yacht club symbol. A pretty moth-eaten type really.

Romeo-y-Cohiba
Well thanks a lot, sweetheart.

Nutscracker
I suspect someone might just have recognised himself. Right, Romeo?

Romeo-y-Cohiba
No one's ever called me a moth-eaten type before. But I do have a tattoo like that on my arm.

Nutscracker
So does anyone have any ideas?

Organizm(-:
I don't get it, are we seriously discussing someone's dream?

UGLI 666
I think . . .

Nutscracker
New members, please introduce yourselves to the group straightaway. What do you think?

UGLI 666
The Lord sent her that vision to make us repent.

Romeo-y-Cohiba
That's just great. We've been locked up in here, and we have to repent? Repent for what?

UGLI 666
What we were locked up for.

Romeo-y-Cohiba
And what were we locked up for?

UGLI 666
Each of us for his own reason. For it is said: 'There
is no man that shall live without sin, though his life
be but a single day.'

Organizm(-:
Ugly, what sex are you?

UGLI 666
That's of no relevance.

Organizm(-:
Is he/she really serious?

Monstradamus
I think he/she means what he/she says.

UGLI 666
I'm female, since it interests you so very much.
My name's xxx, I'm a xxx by profession and a xxx
by education, but by vocation I've always been a
xxx. I've read everything already. And I have nothing interesting to add. As for whether I'm being

serious or not, you can be quite sure I always mean what I say.

Organizm(-:
Tell me, Ugly, did you invent your views to match your name or was your name invented to match your views?

UGLI 666
My name's for my sins. And so is yours.

Organizm(-:
But do you know what 'UGLI' really means? It's not from the word 'ugly' as you probably thought. It's 'Universal Gate for Logic Implementation'. A universal logic element, I remember that from school. So if you chose your views to match your name you were looking in the wrong place altogether.

Monstradamus
We were talking about Ariadne's dream. It has been suggested that she was shown it specially and it contains information for everyone.

Romeo-y-Cohiba

What does that mean – shown it specially? This isn't a cinema. And if the information's for everyone, then why was it shown to Ariadne?

Organizm(-:

You'll get a showing too, don't be in such a hurry.

Romeo-y-Cohiba

You think that monster in the bronze helmet really is walking about outside our doors?

UGLI 666

You don't have to take everything so literally. In the dream the door was made of wood, with a bull's head. But in here it's made of bronze, with an infernal symbol. Dreams are metaphorical.

IsoldA

Ariadne saw Romeo in her dream and when she described him he recognised himself. What kind of metaphor is that?

Romeo-y-Cohiba
Who says I recognised myself? It was just a couple of details that matched.

IsoldA
But what kind of details? There can't be many tattoos like that. An anchor with a dollar sign.

Romeo-y-Cohiba
Let's introduce a bit of clarity here. I actually do have a tattoo on my arm, just above the wrist. It's a fountain of oil, gushing up through a dollar sign. From upside down it looks a bit like an anchor. That's all. I don't know what tattoo she saw. And my yacht club symbol is nothing like that.

Sartrik
xxx me, a xxx sailor.

Nutscracker
New members, once again, please introduce yourselves.

Sartrik

I'm absolutely xxx. My entire body aches.

Monstradamus

Have you been beaten up, or what?

Sartrik

I feel sick. Is there any beer to be had around here?

Monstradamus

I doubt it. Did you overdo it yesterday then?

Sartrik

Something of the sort.

Nutscracker

How did you end up in here?

Sartrik

I don't remember a thing.

Romeo-y-Cohiba

Leave the man alone, let him get his head together.

But can this dream of Ariadne's be interpreted scientifically? Seems to me Monstradamus knows about that kind of thing.

Monstradamus
What does 'interpreted scientifically' mean?

Romeo-y-Cohiba
Well, for instance, this Asterisk is tall, with a big helmet. That symbolises the male sexual organ in a state of erection.

Organizm(-:
And the two dwarves symbolise the balls, do they?

Nutscracker
Cool it, Romeo. Sometimes a *cochiba*'s just a cigar.

IsoldA
Could you talk about that separately somehow?

UGLI 666
I second that motion.

Organizm(-:
Unfortunately we can't just go out into the corridor.

Romeo-y-Cohiba
You didn't answer the question, Monstradamus. Can the dream be analysed?

Monstradamus
If you're thinking of penis symbolism, then I've got nothing to add to what Nutcracker said. But I do have a few observations along an entirely different line. I can share them if you're interested.

Nutscracker
Of course we're interested.

Monstradamus
In the first place, the names. Has anyone any guesses on that score?

UGLI 666
Names of demons from hell.

Monstradamus

The soap, the toilet paper and other items in the bathroom are all marked with something that looks like the symbol for indicating a footnote – a little star. It's called an asterisk, which is also the name of the character Ariadne dreamed about. It sounds a lot like 'Asterius'.

UGLI 666

What's 'Asterius'?

Monstradamus

'Starry' in Latin. Asterius, the son of Minos and Parsiphae. The half-man, half-animal from Crete. Better known as the Minotaur.

Sartrik

That one on the 'Remy Martin' bottle?

Organizm(-:

No, the 'Remy Martin' beast is a Cyclops. The Minotaur is a freak with a bull's head.

Sartrik
God, I feel really sick.

Monstradamus
Now for that double axe on the door. In Greek it's called a 'labros'. That's where we get the word 'Labyrinth', the place where the Minotaur lived. Some accounts say it was a beautiful palace with lots of corridors and rooms, according to others it was a foul-smelling cave with numerous branches plunged in eternal darkness. Or it could be that people from different cultures had different impressions of the same place.

IsoldA
But what has an axe got to do with a labyrinth?

Monstradamus
They find them in Crete. Where the labyrinth was. That's all I know.

UGLI 666
Maybe the Minotaur was killed with an axe like that?

Monstradamus

Let me go on with the names. As well as Asterius and Asterisk, it's hard not to notice another coincidence. It was Ariadne who dreamed about him. That was the name of the Minotaur's sister. And it was also Ariadne who started this thread with the question about the labyrinth.

IsoldA

It's a very common name. I had a lotion for dry skin called 'Ariadne's Milk'.

Romeo-y-Cohiba

Names and coincidences are all very well. But what I don't understand is – what are we going to do?

Monstradamus

Well, what can we do? Wait for Theseus, who will lead us out of the labyrinth. And hope the joke doesn't go too far.

UGLI 666

Does it seem like a joke to you?

Monstradamus
Well, I'd say our hosts certainly seem to have a sense of humour.

Romeo-y-Cohiba
I haven't laughed even once yet.

Nutscracker
Monster's right. There's definitely humour in all of this, only it's infernal humour. Forcing serious people like us to call each other by idiotic names. Dressing us in ancient Greek *chitons* and making us sit at these screens. And then the Internet we end up in has about as much to do with the real one as we do with Ancient Greece.

Organizm(-:
It's not really all that different. The screen design is an imitation of the 'Guardian' site. The heading is the same – 'Guardian Unlimited'. And the chat area looks the same. The difference is there are hundreds of threads there. But we've only got one.

Monstradamus
The name makes sense though. Our Guardian really is unlimited.

Nutscracker
And another joke is the Merrill Lynch symbol on the flag.

Organizm(-:
But Ariadne saw the flag in a dream, so it's not clear whose joke it is. Our moderators' or hers.

Monstradamus
I wouldn't like to alarm anyone, but shouldn't we consider the possibility that Ariadne herself is also a joke by our moderators, as Organism called them.

Organizm(-:
Why's that?

Monstradamus
Because, phenomenologically speaking, she only

exists in the form of messages of unknown origin signed 'Ariadne'.

Ariadne
Thanks. Ariadne.

Monstradamus
Ariadne, please don't take offence. I'm talking about a hypothetical possibility. It doesn't mean I suspect you of anything. The same thing could apply to any of us.

Organizm(-:
What does 'phenomenologically' mean?

Monstradamus
It's the way you can see these words now.

Ariadne
Everything I told you was the truth.

Nutscracker
Nobody ever doubted it. Nebuchadnezzar's just theorising, right?

Monstradamus
I'm not Nebuchadnezzar.

Nutscracker
Sorry, Monstradamus.

Monstradamus
I'm no more Monstradamus than I am Nebuchadnezzar, so what's the difference?

Organizm(-:
You know what I think? Either no one's noticed it or everyone has, but no one's saying.

Romeo-y-Cohiba
What's that, then?

Organizm(-:
We don't post our messages complete, like in a normal chat room. The words appear on the screen one letter at a time, in real time. We can even interrupt each other, and then three dots appear at the end of the phrase that's interrupted.

Nutscracker
Everyone's noticed that.

Organizm(-:
But at the same time, as far as I can tell, no one's made a single spelling mistake yet. Not a single typing error. Doesn't that seem a bit strange?

Monstradamus
That's richt.

Nutscracker
They cantroll our entire canvasation.

IsoldA
Are yew ploying the foul?

Romeo-y-Cohiba
No, I woodn't deram of it.

Monstradamus
Me kneether. It's the mooderattors.

Romeo-y-Cohiba

Step mucking us, you ratten scam!

UGLI 666

There's no point in getting upset, Romeo. It won't help matters.

IsoldA

Have they really stopped?

Organizm(-:

Good for you, Romeo! They did what you told them to. Why not try telling our moderators to do something else?

Romeo-y-Cohiba

Stick your xxx up your xxx and give it a double right twist.

IsoldA

They're following every word we write.

Monstradamus
Maybe that's why Theseus isn't saying anything?

Organizm(-:
What Theseus?

Nutscracker
The one who killed the Minotaur, Organism. Or who has to kill him. What do you have in mind, Monstradamus?

Monstradamus
Maybe he's already here, but he doesn't want the moderator to notice him. And I suspect the moderator's our bronze mushroom.

Romeo-y-Cohiba
You talk about him as if you'd seen him with your own eyes. But we don't actually have any reason to believe he exists.

Ariadne
Who do you mean? Theseus or Asterisk?

Romeo-y-Cohiba
Both.

Monstradamus
And for exactly the same reason, Romeo, there's no reason to believe that you exist.

Romeo-y-Cohiba
That just about does it. Leave it out, will you?

Ariadne
Perhaps Theseus is one of us?

Nutscracker
Perhaps the Minotaur's one of us.

Organizm(-:
I bet a hundred xxx the Minotaur's Monstradamus.

Monstradamus
Stop clowning about.

Organizm(-:
Theseus, answer us!

IsoldA
At least tell us if you're here or not! Theseus!

Monstradamus
By the way. If the moderators can fulfil our wishes, why don't we ask them to open the door?

UGLI 666
But what's outside the door?

Organizm(-:
We can find out.

Romeo-y-Cohiba
You be careful, or the door might really go ahead and open.

Ariadne
I've composed a little poem. Dedicated to Monstradamus.

Monstradamus
Let's hear it.

Ariadne
The Minotaur lurks at the door,
His axe it gleams moon-bright.
'Dear Watson this could not be more . . .'
Then silence in the night.

Monstradamus
A bit on the dark side. But maybe I deserve it for
being so suspicious.

Organizm(-:
An experiment. Doors, open!

UGLI 666
Lord have mercy!

Romeo-y-Cohiba
I warned you!

Ariadne
Did it happen in all the rooms?

Monstradamus
It did in mine.

UGLI 666
Do you mean the music or the door?

Ariadne
The whole thing at once.

IsoldA
I've got sky outside. Grey. Looks a bit like a park.
Everything seems quiet. I'm going out to explore.

Romeo-y-Cohiba
Hey, Isolde, wait! It could be dangerous out
there!

UGLI 666
It's dark out there.

Romeo-y-Cohiba
Isolde!

Nutscracker
Did everyone hear the trumpets?

Ariadne
Do you think they were trumpets?

Organizm(-:
Doors, close!

Nutscracker
xxx be praised.

Monstradamus
Organizm, don't go trying any more experiments like
that.

Romeo-y-Cohiba
Now how's Isolde going to get back? Doors, open!

Nutscracker

xxx, eh? Again!

Monstradamus

Let's just keep calm and get our bearings.

Organizm(-:

Okay, I think I've got it. When the door opens, a lever shaped like a leg with a hoof moves out and down.

UGLI 666

Lord save us and keep us!

Nutscracker

To make the door close, you push the lever. To make it open, you press on the axe in the middle. So everyone can open their own door when they want to.

Romeo-y-Cohiba

It works.

Monstradamus

What can you see outside the door?

Ariadne
There's another room outside mine.

UGLI 666
Semi-darkness. Benches, a lot of benches.

Romeo-y-Cohiba
Fresh air at last.

Sartrik
Two fridges full of booze. So there is a God after all!

Organizm(-:
Plywood walls painted to look like bricks. It all looks pretty naff.

Nutscracker
I've got a load of electronic equipment.

Organizm(-:
I'm hungry. Hey, you moderators, how's about a bit of nosh down here? Right . . . I think I've

got it. You have to turn this thingy that way, and then that thingy this way . . . Now we're talking.

Monstradamus
What?

Romeo-y-Cohiba
What was it you turned, tell us.

Organizm(-:
They sent down some pancakes with jam. Not bad for Ancient Greece. I feel like a nice quiet meal, so I'm taking a break now.

Romeo-y-Cohiba
Enjoy your meal. Just tell us what it was you turned.

Organizm(-:
When I'm feeding my tum, I go all deaf and dumb.

Ariadne
Organism, you only need to type two words! Then you can go ahead and eat in peace.

Nutscracker
Organism, we're all asking you.

Organizm(-:
I'm busy.

UGLI 666
I never understood before why gluttony is a sin. Then a spiritual friend of mine explained. Gluttony is not so very terrible in itself. But it's a sign of a base soul. The same thing applies to debauchery. The soul doesn't become debased through committing these acts. A base soul manifests itself through them.

Romeo-y-Cohiba
No, you won't get under his skin that easily.

Monstradamus
Moderators! Give us all something to eat!

Ariadne
I heard some kind of noise. But where's the food?

Monstradamus
There's a small flap to the right of the monitor. Just a rectangle in the wall. Lift the flap and you'll find a tray behind it.

Ariadne
I found it, thank you.

Romeo-y-Cohiba
But what are you supposed to turn? Organism said . . .

Ariadne
He was just joking, Romeo. Having a laugh.

Nutscracker
Let's all eat in peace. *Bon appetit*.

IsoldA
I'm back. Who's there?

Romeo-y-Cohiba
I am. Is everything all right?

IsoldA
Yes.

Romeo-y-Cohiba
I was worried.

IsoldA
I was only gone for a moment. Where's everyone else?

Romeo-y-Cohiba
They're eating. There's just the two of us.

IsoldA
What's outside your door?

Romeo-y-Cohiba
A labyrinth of neatly trimmed rough bushes higher than my head. And running between the bushes is a dirt pathway.

IsoldA
And I've got the same kind of bushes along the sides of an alley.

Romeo-y-Cohiba
An alley?

IsoldA
My door opens into a park. The alley starts right outside and along the sides there are bushes. With treetops showing above them in places.

Romeo-y-Cohiba
What I've got is more like a corridor between the bushes, I wouldn't call it an alley. And it starts winding straightaway, so I can't see anything but leaves. It's more like a narrow corridor than anything else, neatly sliced through the bushes by something like a combine harvester.

IsoldA
What colour is the ground there?

Romeo-y-Cohiba
Beige.

IsoldA
It's beige here too. We're near each other!

Romeo-y-Cohiba
What else did you see?

IsoldA
I didn't go very far. There are lots of alleys, and they keep branching and twisting and turning corners. I wasn't afraid in the least. Quite the opposite, what I saw gave me a really good feeling. The labyrinth might be complex, but it's impossible to get lost in.

Romeo-y-Cohiba
Why?

IsoldA
Because there's a plan hanging at every place the path branches. And there's a little sign on the plan: 'You are here'.

Romeo-y-Cohiba
That's handy all right. And wasn't there any little sign saying: 'The Minotaur is here'?

IsoldA
No.

Romeo-y-Cohiba
I was joking. Did you meet anyone?

IsoldA
No. But several times I had the feeling there was someone just round the corner.

Romeo-y-Cohiba
And was there anything like what Ariadne was talking about?

IsoldA
Yes, kind of. Only not exactly. Once I spotted some roofs above the bushes, but they were a long way off. And I saw fountains with different kinds of figures.

Romeo-y-Cohiba
Like the one Ariadne talked about?

IsoldA
I don't know. I went through a few forks in the path and at every one there was a small . . . I don't know what to call it – an oasis, I suppose. Trees and a fountain with bronze figures of animals. First a hare and a tortoise. They were sitting facing each other, with their faces lifted up to the sky. Their mouths were open and there were long thin streams of water spurting out. To be quite honest, it looked a bit ridiculous, as though they were spitting at an invisible ceiling that was too high, so that everything just fell back down on their own heads. At another fork there was a fountain with a fox and a crow. The crow was high up in the tree, and so big it looked more like an eagle. There was a water pipe leading up to it, hidden among the leaves. The fox was squatting on his haunches gazing up at the crow as though it was trying to hit it with the stream of water spurting out of its throat, but it couldn't reach high enough. The crow had its wings pulled back and up

and its beak was open, and there was another stream of water spurting out of that, as though the sight of the fox made it feel sick.

Sartrik
Now that's something I can understand.

IsoldA
What do you understand?

Romeo-y-Cohiba
Take no notice. You're a wonderful storyteller, Isolde. It was like seeing it all with my own eyes.

IsoldA
Yes, I forgot to say. The plan that was hanging everywhere looked more like an old engraving than something modern. Or like an enlarged photocopy of an engraving. And written on it in this strange oblique typeface was: *plan du labirinthe de versailles.* What could that mean? Is it from the word 'verse'? Because there are characters from fables in the fountains?

Romeo-y-Cohiba

A plan of the labyrinth at Versailles. That's a real piece of luck.

IsoldA

Versailles? Then why is it written with a small letter?

Monstradamus

I could suggest that's not really the strangest thing about our surroundings.

Romeo-y-Cohiba

Do you mind not butting into other people's conversations?

Monstradamus

Sorry, I didn't realise it was private.

IsoldA

And where did you go, Romeo?

Romeo-y-Cohiba

I haven't been outside yet.

IsoldA

Why not?

Romeo-y-Cohiba

I think it's some kind of trap.

IsoldA

I think it's a trap, too. But we're already caught in it anyway. And the room you're sitting in is just as much a part of it as what's outside the door.

Romeo-y-Cohiba

That's true. I suppose I ought to go out and scout around. Maybe I could find the way to your fountains.

IsoldA

Wait, Romeo. It's dark out there already. You can go tomorrow. Why don't you tell me what you look like instead? Are you like what Ariadne said?

Romeo-y-Cohiba

I don't understand why everyone's decided I was the man she dreamed about. The only things we have in common are the tattoo and the moustache. We've already dealt with the tattoo. That just leaves the moustache. And that's like identifying a man by the colour of his tie.

IsoldA
Are you really bald?

Romeo-y-Cohiba
Not bald, my head's shaved. That's a big difference. People go bald because they have no choice, but they shave their heads out of self-respect. Even if it does look the same from a distance. And my mole is really small, you can hardly see it. And anyway, who doesn't have some kind of a mole on his face?

IsoldA
Are you handsome?

Romeo-y-Cohiba
What does 'handsome' mean?

IsoldA

Well, it means a man is nice to look at.

Romeo-y-Cohiba

Nice for who? I got used to the way I look ages ago. And as far as anyone else is concerned, it depends on the circumstances. But one thing I can say for certain is you needn't be afraid of being with me.

IsoldA

What do you mean? Do you mean I wouldn't be frightened of you? Or do you mean that with you I wouldn't have to be afraid of anything?

Nutscracker

He's trying to say that if you're with him even he won't frighten you.

Romeo-y-Cohiba

Just give people a chance to talk, will you? Isolde, can I ask you something about yourself?

IsoldA
Such as?

Romeo-y-Cohiba
Such as . . . Do you like poetry?

IsoldA
Sometimes.

Romeo-y-Cohiba
Who's your favourite poet?

IsoldA
Caroline Kennedy.

Romeo-y-Cohiba
What has she written?

IsoldA
'The Favourite Poems of Jacqueline Kennedy-Onassis.'

Romeo-y-Cohiba
And what do you look like?

IsoldA
How would you like me to look?

Romeo-y-Cohiba
I'd like to know how you really look.

IsoldA
Medium height. Dark hair. Green eyes. They say I'm beautiful.

Romeo-y-Cohiba
But can you describe yourself so I can imagine how you look?

IsoldA
I have been told . . . But I'm not sure it's worth mentioning.

Romeo-y-Cohiba
What have you been told?

IsoldA
I was compared once to a cover of 'The New Yorker'

that had a drawing of Monica Lewinsky as the Mona Lisa. Only I look five times younger.

Romeo-y-Cohiba
You mean you look like Monica Lewinsky?

IsoldA
No, not at all.

Romeo-y-Cohiba
Like the Mona Lisa then?

IsoldA
Not in the slightest. I suppose it sounds stupid.

Romeo-y-Cohiba
It sounds just fine. I just don't quite get it.

Monstradamus
Allow me to explain. There was nothing mysterious about Monica Lewinsky, and nothing sexual about the Mona Lisa. But if we imagine the scintillating mystery of the Mona Lisa fused with the earthy

sensuality of Monica Lewinsky, and then add the charm of early youth, we get Isolde. Get it now?

Romeo-y-Cohiba

How many damn times do I have to tell you not to go butting into other people's conversations, Nebuchadnezzar?

Monstradamus

I'm not Nebuchadnezzar.

Romeo-y-Cohiba

Don't butt in anyway. I thought you wanted to eat. So why don't you?

Monstradamus

I've already eaten.

Romeo-y-Cohiba

Then have something to drink. Isolde, they won't give us any peace.

IsoldA

It's late already. Let's go to bed.

Romeo-y-Cohiba

OK. See you tomorrow, if it ever comes.

IsoldA

Let's hope it does. Ah yes, something else I forgot to tell you. I braid my hair at the back.

Ariadne

I think they're in love.

Monstradamus

According to their names they have to be. Imagine being called Romeo. What else could you do?

Organizm(-:

Take a pack of condoms and go looking for your Juliet.

Nutscracker

Or take a pump-action shotgun and go looking for your Shakespeare.

Romeo-y-Cohiba
Just leave it out, can't you?

Nutscracker
Romeo, are you still there? We thought you'd gone
to bed.

Monstradamus
Ariadne! If you dream about that bronze mushroom
again, try to find out what he's got on his mind.

:-))

Monstradamus
Ariadne, are you awake already?

Ariadne
Where are all the others?

Monstradamus
I don't know. Sleeping, I suppose. Well then? Did you
dream about anything?

Ariadne

Yes.

Monstradamus

Tell me about it.

Ariadne

It was like a lecture. I was sitting in a lecture hall in some educational institution – a technical college to judge from all the pieces of equipment standing along the walls. I can't say what kind of equipment it was, some pieces had screens like televisions, others looked like scales with a lot of springs and counterweights. The lecture hall looked like an amphitheatre – it sloped down to a board and standing there beside it was the same dwarf who spoke to me by the fountain. Apart from us two, there was no one there. The entire board was covered by a complicated diagram of some kind of device.

Monstradamus

Can you remember what came before that? How you got there?

Ariadne

No. The dwarf waved to me as if I was an old friend and told me they had heard about our wish to discover what was on their master's mind. He said that would be the subject of the lecture. Everything that happened seemed to be perfectly natural, and I didn't feel like I needed to ask any questions. Although there were lots of strange things. For instance, the diagram wasn't drawn on the board with chalk. It was carved into it, like an engraving. I realised that because when the dwarf wanted to correct something in the drawing he took a chisel and began stripping long shavings of plastic off the board and leaving bright lines on it.

Monstradamus

What was it a diagram of?

Ariadne

It was Asterisk's mind.

Monstradamus

His mind?

Ariadne

Yes. The diagram was called 'the helmet of horror' – it was written in big letters above the drawing. But the dwarf repeated very insistently several times that it wasn't any kind of hat or apparatus, but precisely a mind, although everything about it looked like a drawing of some machine. The main body of the machine was shaped like a helmet. And there was an identical helmet standing on the demonstration table – an ancient bronze headpiece, and underneath it a visor with holes in it curving back inside.

Monstradamus

What do you mean by 'curving back inside'?

Ariadne

Its lower section ran back inside the helmet through a slit in the middle of the face. And there were some kind of side plates too – everything was very old, green with age. It looked like a Roman gladiator's helmet – like a bronze hat with a visor. Only this one had horns as well. They came out of the upper section of the helmet and curved backwards. I'd already seen that on the square by the fountain, when Asterisk walked by, only his helmet was bigger and more complicated, with lots of different wires and tubes. The dwarf said this one was a simplified model. What he told me sounded really peculiar.

Monstradamus
Can you tell me about it?

Ariadne
I remember that the helmet of horror consisted of several major parts and a lot of secondary ones. The parts had strange names: the frontal net, the now grid, the separator labyrinth, the horns of plenty, Tarkovsky's mirror and so forth. The largest element consisted of the now grid and the frontal net. It had two parts that were sometimes fused into a single unit. Its external part, the net, looked like a visor with holes in it, and its internal part, the grid, divided the helmet into an upper section and a lower one, so there was no way you could squeeze even the smallest head into it. The dwarf said the now grid separates the past from the present, because it

is the only place where what we call 'now' exists. Hence the name. The past is located in the upper section of the helmet, and the future in the lower section.

Monstradamus
That doesn't seem logical somehow. Maybe it's the other way round?

Ariadne
No, I definitely remember that. After that the dwarf began explaining how the helmet works. He said you had to grasp the essence of the matter first before going into the details. The helmet's operating cycle has no beginning, so it can be explained starting from any phase. And so, he said, start by imagining the gentle glow of a summer day caressing your face. That's precisely how the frontal net, heated by the action of the stream of impressions falling on it, transmits heat to the now grid. The grid sublimates the past contained in the upper section of the helmet, transforming it into vapour, which is driven up into the horns of plenty by the force of circumstances.

The horns of plenty emerge from the forehead, curve round the sides of the helmet and intertwine to form the occipital braid, which descends into the base of the helmet. There, below the now grid, the bubbles of hope that arise in the occipital braid are ejected into the region of the future. As they rise, these bubbles burst against the now grid, generating the force of circumstances, which induces the stream of impressions in the separator labyrinth. And the stream of impressions, in turn, is shattered against the frontal net, heating the now grid and renewing the energy of the cycle. The heat he was speaking about when he used the verb 'to heat' is different from the kind of heat you get from fire, more like the kind you get from love. He said he was simply using an analogy with something I knew about, so I would be able to imagine what happens. And in the same way the stream of impressions doesn't actually flow anywhere, the bubbles of hope aren't really bubbles at all, and so on.

Monstradamus
I couldn't really say I understood all of that.

Ariadne

I didn't understand anything at first either, and the dwarf told me to ask questions. I didn't know where to begin, because everything was equally hard to understand. The last thing he'd mentioned was the bubbles of hope, so I asked why they were called that. The dwarf was a bit embarrassed and said it was the official name, like a formal title. In actual fact it's not always hope at all, he said, it's more likely to be fear and apprehension, suspicion and hate, all sorts of nonsense, in fact any of the cud that is chewed on with such habitual stupidity by . . . But then he broke off, glanced round furtively and muttered something about that not being the right way to put it. And then he went on in the formal lecturer's voice he'd been using before and said that technically speaking it was correct to call them bubbles of the past. And they were called bubbles because their constant tendency is to expand and occupy the entire volume of the helmet, preventing anything else from appearing in it and leaving no space or opportunity for the recognition of what is actually happening. The dwarf jabbed his pointer at the part of the diagram that showed the kind of vertical coil the horns formed where they came together at the back of the helmet and said that bubbles of hope arise in the occipital braid following the enrichment of past in the horns of plenty. But since past is enriched exclusively with more past, the bubbles of hope consist entirely of past, they are simply past in a different state. Which means that when Asterisk peers into the future, he sees nothing but the past. The lower section of the helmet is required primarily in order to cool the bubbles of hope, a process which endows them with vernal freshness and the elastic resilience of novelty. As they break against the now grid, they generate the force of circumstances, which lifts the past out of the upper section of the helmet into the entry chamber of the horns of plenty and forces it through the separator labyrinth, where the stream of impressions arises.

Monstradamus
What is the separator labyrinth?

Ariadne
It's a kind of plate with wavy slits in it located in the

region of the forehead, in front of the entry chamber of the horns of plenty. The separator labyrinth is the most important part of the helmet of horror. It's the place where everything else is produced out of nothing, that is, the place where the stream of impressions arises. And it's also the place where the past, the present and the future are separated. The past moves upwards, the future moves downwards, and the present, in the form of the stream of impressions, falls on to the outer surface of the frontal net, generating the cycle's passionate desire to recur, so that it becomes a kind of *perpetuum mobile*.

Monstradamus

Hang on a moment. The bubbles of hope are just another state of past, right?

Ariadne

Yes, that's the way I understood it.

Monstradamus

But after they break, you get past, present and future?

Ariadne
That's right.

Monstradamus
That means it's past that decomposes into past, present and future?

Ariadne
In actual fact the whole cycle is simply the circulation of now in various states of mind, in the same way that water can be ice, or the sea, or thirst.

Monstradamus
But how does the stream of impressions arise in the separator labyrinth?

Ariadne
Under the force of circumstances.

Monstradamus
I see. But no, hang on. The separator labyrinth is inside the helmet?

Ariadne
Yes.

Monstradamus
You said the stream of impressions falls on to the
outer surface of the helmet. But how can that
happen, if it arises inside?

Ariadne
I asked about that too. The dwarf laughed and said
that was merely an apparent contradiction. The
point is, he explained, the 'inside' and 'outside' I was
talking about have no existence in themselves. They
are generated in the separator labyrinth by the force
of circumstances and from there they enter the horns
of plenty, where they enrich the past, transforming
it into the state of bubbles of hope. But since there
is no 'inside' and 'outside' anywhere except in the
horns of plenty, the stream of impressions can quite
easily arise inside the helmet and fall on to it from
the outside. And the same applies to everything else
as well. But the dwarf warned me that I should never
under any circumstances regard anything as real. The

entire phenomenon is induced, like the electromagnetic field in a transformer.

Monstradamus
Aha. Then what is Tarkovsky's mirror?

Ariadne
It's a small, fogged-up mirror set at an angle of forty degrees between the region of the future and the now grid. When the bubbles of hope entering from below are reflected in it they appear to be further along the line of their course than they are, which gives rise to the feeling that the line actually exists.

Monstradamus
I see. And why is the separator labyrinth the most important section of the structure?

Ariadne
Firstly, it's where the stream of impressions arises. Secondly, it's where 'I' and 'you', good and bad, right and left, black and white, so on and so forth and everything else arises. The dwarf said this part of the

helmet of horror is the most important and it hasn't changed for thousands and thousands of years. Then just at that moment a ray of sunlight lit up a poster hanging beside the board. It showed a Cretan coin with a diagram of a labyrinth stamped into it. Most opportune, said the dwarf, that *is* the separator labyrinth. Its appearance is very distinctive. It has a cross section at the centre, which is reached immediately after entry, and numerous parallel paths running around the cross which seem at first to lead you off into the unknown but then come full circle. This is the most widespread image of the labyrinth, the one that is repeated on almost all the antique coins and drawings. The scanned projection of this labyrinth is a straight line, which means that once you've entered it there's no way you can get lost or find your way out. And that means we can regard the horns of plenty, the now grid, the separator labyrinth, the past and future as different sections of one and the same continuous route, which no one is actually following.

Monstradamus
Why are the horns of plenty called that?

Ariadne

Because they contain all sorts of everything – tender feelings, sidelong glances, exalted words, final thoughts and everything else. A genuine treasure house or rubbish tip. But all this infinite variety actually consists entirely of past. As far as I could understand it, the horns of plenty operate like enrichment units in a chemical plant. When it's driven through them by the force of circumstances, past gets mixed up with everything else, becoming richer and acquiring value, with the result that bubbles of hope are produced in the occipital braid, go gurgling through the region of the future, are reflected in Tarkovsky's mirror and perceived as the novel freshness of a brand new day.

Monstradamus

For a while now I've been getting the feeling something's not right here, but I just can't quite put my finger on it. Right, now I think I've got it! Who are they perceived by?

Ariadne

Who? By Asterisk, of course.

Monstradamus

That's it! But where is he, this Asterisk? The way I understand it, this helmet is arranged so you can't even squeeze your fist inside it, never mind your head. I don't suppose you asked about that?

Ariadne

No, I didn't, the dwarf told me himself. Asterisk comes into being in the same place as everything else. In the separator labyrinth.

Monstradamus

And then what?

Ariadne

And then the force of circumstances induces him to enter the horns of plenty, he gets mixed up with everything else, is enriched and returns to the now grid in the form of bubbles of hope.

Monstradamus

You don't understand. I want to know about the subject of perception of all this xxx. Its ultimate subject. Can't you understand that? Where is he?

Ariadne
I really don't understand what an ultimate subject of perception is. But there can't be any doubt that he must be in the horns of plenty, because there just isn't anywhere else.

Monstradamus
Then where does he come from?

Ariadne
From the separator labyrinth. Like everything else.

Monstradamus
Then what's the point of the whole business?

Ariadne
I don't know.

Monstradamus
All right. Let's try it a step at a time. Where does perception arise?

Ariadne
It's produced in the separator labyrinth.

Monstradamus
From what?

Ariadne
From the past. It was there in the past, wasn't it?

Monstradamus
It was.

Ariadne
Then why should it suddenly disappear from the present and the future?

Monstradamus
Where's Nutcracker got to? I can't make sense of all this on my own.

Nutscracker
I'm following your discussion with intense interest.

Monstradamus

My helmet of horror's about to overheat. Let me put the question a different way. If Asterisk, perception and everything else are produced in the separator labyrinth, then why do we say that it's Asterisk who perceives them?

Ariadne

The dwarf said that is simply his specific quality as a product. In other words, the idea that he perceives everything is produced in the separator labyrinth together with everything else.

Nutscracker

Produced from what?

Ariadne

From nothing. You haven't been listening properly.

Nutscracker

All right. Then I have a question as well. You say Asterisk appears in the separator labyrinth.

Ariadne

That's right.

Nutscracker

And instead of a head he has the helmet of horror?

Ariadne

Yes.

Nutscracker

But then that means the helmet of horror appears in the separator labyrinth, which is located inside the helmet itself?

Ariadne

Yes, it does.

Nutscracker

But the helmet has to be bigger than one of its parts. How can it be located inside one of its own components?

Ariadne

The dwarf said 'inside' and 'outside' only exist in the horns of plenty. The same thing applies to 'bigger' and 'smaller'. The horns contain absolutely everything you could possibly imagine and everything else as well.

Nutscracker

But in that case even the helmet only exists in these horns of plenty?

Ariadne

Yes, I think so.

Nutscracker

Whichever way you look at it, that means the helmet of horror arises inside one of its own component parts. But it exists inside a different one. Where's the sense in that?

Ariadne

Where? In the horns of plenty, of course.

Nutscracker

Ariadne, are you serious?

Ariadne

Yes, probably. Or perhaps not. To be quite honest, I'm tired. If I meet the dwarf, I'll make sure I ask him about everything. You think up some questions.

Monstradamus

Hang on a moment. How did the dream end?

Ariadne

After the lecture I went out into the corridor. There was no one there, just a big mirror in a semicircular frame on the wall. I went over and looked into it and woke up.

Monstradamus

What did you see in it?

Ariadne
Myself.

Monstradamus

And nothing unusual?

Ariadne

I was wearing a straw hat with a round crown and two little bunches of lilies-of-the-valley pinned to the brim at the back. The hat had a veil of thick lace with round holes, so I couldn't see my face behind it at all. It all looked very beautiful, but something made me feel nervous. I couldn't work out what was wrong until suddenly I recognised that bronze mask in my reflection and that frightened me, and then the dream suddenly ended. That's all. I'm going.

Organizm(-:

I thought from the very beginning that goon must be wearing a virtual reality helmet. Honest I did.

Nutscracker

That's not any kind of virtual reality helmet; it's some kind of fancy pressure cooker. Games for children. I ought to know how a virtual reality helmet works when grown-ups put one together, and this is nothing like it.

Organizm(-:
And how does it work?

Nutscracker
Maybe I don't understand too well which way the current flows and what it's transformed into and all, but I do know perfectly well what someone in one of those helmets sees and thinks, because I've dealt with it as a professional, by studying the problem of choice in an interactive environment. We worked with those helmets all the time.

Organizm(-:
I've never heard of that problem. What is it?

Nutscracker
Well, imagine you decide for yourself who's going to shoot who when you're watching an action movie. If you decide the main hero gets killed in the first shoot-out, then what happens to the rest of the plot? If you had genuinely free choice, the results could be pretty miserable. But art is supposed to make us happy, not miserable.

Monstradamus

That's for sure. And even when it does make us miserable, we should feel happy in our misery.

Nutscracker

That's right! So there never is any genuine interactivity, only the appearance of it. Or rather, it is permitted, but only within a narrow range where no choice you make can change the fundamental situation. The main problem is to eliminate freedom of choice so that the subject is led unerringly to make the decision required, while at the same time maintaining his firm belief that his choice is free. In scientific terms it's known as coercive orientation.

UGLI 666

What's that?

Nutscracker

That's a long story.

Organizm(-:

We don't have much else to occupy ourselves with.

Monstradamus

That's right. Tell us about it, Nutcracker. Let's give our brains a break.

Nutscracker

I suppose there's no need to explain what the Helmholtz sees?

Organizm(-:

Who?

Nutscracker

In professional jargon that's what they call the guy in the helmet. A Helmholtz is someone who's located in an artificial dimension that totally isolates him from the real world and moves around in it, or rather, thinks he moves around in it. Let's assume this dimension takes the form of a flat area with three identical marble vases standing on it. And what we have to do to keep the action moving in the right direction is to lead the Helmholtz to the middle vase.

Organizm(-:
Three identical marble vases. Hardly makes it worth bothering to put the helmet on.

Nutscracker
Instead of vases they could be doors, turns at a road junction, any kind of choice at all in fact. It's not important. Everything you see in the helmet is computed by a special program and the program can be set up so that, every time, the Helmholtz makes the same choice we made for him earlier.

Organizm(-:
Sure, you can fix the program, but not the experimental subject. He's got his own programming.

Nutscracker
That's the whole point. When the helmet and the Helmholtz fuse into a single whole, you can edit the reader as well as the book, if you get my meaning. That's why we say editing technology can be external or internal. Although there's no clear boundary between them, of course.

Organizm(-:
Come again?

Nutscracker
External technologies affect what we see, internal technologies affect what we think.

Organizm(-:
How about an example?

Nutscracker
The simplest external editing program is 'Sticky Eye'. That's when, as you turn your head, one of the vases gets stuck in the field of vision and lingers there longer than it should.

Monstradamus
But what about the two other vases? They're standing next to it. According to the laws of perspective . . .

Nutscracker
How perspective operates inside the helmet is decided by us and our client. Another method is

called 'The Weight'. When the Helmholtz tries to move away from our vase, the program slows down his movement. And when he approaches, it speeds his movement up. As though we've tied a mathematical weight to his foot and it keeps disappearing and reappearing again. That makes it easier to move towards the chosen vase than in any other direction, and disorganised series of random displacements will bring the Helmholtz to it pretty quickly.

Organizm(-:
A mathematical weight. That's beautiful.

Nutscracker
The next technology up is 'Pavlov's Bitch'. That's an intermediate conditioned reflex editor.

Organizm(-:
So it's named after that Russian scientist who noticed his stomach juices started flowing when the phone rang?

UGLI 666

No he didn't, he just studied conditioned reflexes in dogs.

Nutscracker

I didn't invent the name. When you look at the vases that we want to exclude from your list, your vision starts blurring and rippling and you get a horrible buzzing in your ears, or even an electric shock. So you won't look at them again.

UGLI 666

But you'd notice that straightaway.

Nutscracker

We want you to notice it straightaway, draw the right conclusion and look in the right direction in future. It's a cheap technology for third-world countries. But if the budget's big enough, then for instance we can use infrasonics. The Helmholtz won't notice anything, but he'll experience a dark, mysterious horror when he turns towards any vase except the one we want. The obverse method is stimulation of the pleasure centre when the correct choice is made. They used to insert an electrode, but now it's done by pharmacological means or by entraining the brain to delta rhythms.

Organizm(-:
You don't say. Are you telling me they'll be doing all that stuff to us if we watch interactive movies?

Nutscracker
I don't think so. These techniques weren't developed for the movies, not even for virtual spaces. They were just modelled there. The topic is not in the public domain. But since you and I aren't in the public domain either, I suppose it's okay for me to tell you about it.

Organizm(-:
So what are the internal editing programs like?

Nutscracker
Well, for instance, take 'Sunny Kiss'. The vase we have to choose is endowed with positive emotional

coloration by employing universally accepted aesthetic codes, given a positive inner content, if you like.

UGLI 666
Inner content. Would that be inside the vase or inside the viewer?

Nutscracker
That's a difficult question. You could say it's inside the helmet. But all that's just words. It's easier for me to explain how it's done. Say a ray of sunlight falls on our vase, or you hear a soulful melody in the air when it enters your field of view. The reverse technique is 'Doom and Gloom'. For instance, when you look at a vase we don't like, the sun is covered by dark clouds, a grey fog comes down and you hear unpleasant noises.

Organizm(-:
Fair enough. What else?

Nutscracker
There's another technology called 'The Seventh Seal'. The vase that has to be chosen is marked out

using secret signs that attract interest or stimulate the imagination. It can be absolutely anything – a hand print on its surface, arrows pointing to it on the ground, a dove sitting on its edge, mysterious graffiti, and so on and so forth. The obverse method is 'The Le Pen Club'. That's when the vases we wish to exclude are covered in the crudest obscenities you can imagine, preferably not even in paint, but xxx. Virtual, of course.

Organizm(-:
And you mean the Helmholtz won't notice anything?

Nutscracker
Used on its own, any one of the techniques used is easy enough to spot. But if the methods are combined together in a subtle fashion and always applied in rotation at a level of intensity just on the border line of perception, you get practically a hundred per cent precise manipulation combined with total imperceptibility.

Organizm(-:

I get it. It's like what you see at the railway stations in Asia. When a passenger thinks it's the tumbler-gambler who's going to cheat him but actually everyone playing the game is in on the swindle even though they're arguing with each other all the time, maybe even fighting.

Nutscracker

Exactly. Only in our case absolutely everybody in the station is in on it, including the stone Atlantes by the main entrance.

Ariadne

How clever you are, Nutcracker. After I listened to you I wrote a poem. It's dedicated to you, Romeo and Isolde. Shall I read it?

Nutscracker

Go on.

Ariadne

Beyond the window-pane on Doom and Gloom
Old Pavlov's Bitch's Sticky Glance is glued.

My Minotaur! Creep silently into my room
Beckon me with a glance, brazenly nude.

Nutscracker
Powerful as ever. And he's already partly fulfilled your
wish by removing his helmet, even though he has no
head underneath it. I'd say it's impossible to expose
yourself any more brazenly than that.

UGLI 666
Nutscracker, there's one thing about what you say I
can't understand. How can you change what's in front
of a person's eyes without him noticing? If he's looking at the same place but sees something different,
how can he fail to notice?

Nutscracker
I couldn't understand that at first either. But for the
Helmholtz the word 'change' has no meaning. In real
life what you see depends on where you look. But
when you're wearing a helmet, it's the other way
round — where you're looking depends on what you
see. Is that clear?

UGLI 666
Not entirely.

Nutscracker
In the real world you see what's in front of your eyes. No matter which way you point your rump. But in this world you see what's in front of your eyes, no matter which way you point your head. As we used to say in the xxx, it's chalk and cheese, even though it sounds pretty much the same. You don't have any independent system of coordinates, and we decide everything you see. So you can't even suspect anything. For you even the world isn't what it really is, but what's shown to you. You feel like you're looking around in a natural manner, but in fact all the time your eyes keep stumbling over our candidate — sorry, I mean our vase — and it gives you this light and happy feeling. But you never think to ask why, the same way no one ever asks why it's a sunny day.

Organizm(-:
An interesting slip of the tongue.

Nutscracker
And if the mark turns his head too rapidly, so that 'Sticky Eye' and 'Sunny Kiss' stop working, then 'Doom and Gloom' and 'The Weight' kick in immediately.

Organizm(-:
Well, Nutcracker, so now I understand what you do for a living. Tell me, as a professional, do you reckon they could be influencing us in some similar kind of way in here?

Nutscracker
I'd have to think about that.

UGLI 666
I noticed a long time ago that conspiracy theory has taken the place of religion for atheists. They always think there's someone manipulating them, hypnotising them, zombifying them, bugging them, trailing them. But that someone is simply the devil, and that's all. The fact is, it's only a short step from atheism to schizophrenia, and in most

cases it's already been taken. What about you, Organism? Do you feel like someone's manipulating you?

Organizm(-:
To be honest, I do.

UGLI 666
What kind of manipulation is it?

Organizm(-:
Being locked in here, for instance. Or being fed pancakes for the second day running.

UGLI 666
Ah, in that sense. But that's not manipulation, that's God's punishment.

Organizm(-:
Ugly, let me explain to you how we're manipulated in here. Let's assume that headgear on Asterisk's head is a virtual reality helmet after all.

UGLI 666
And then what?

Organizm(-:
Perhaps everything we see here is something like that flat area Nutcracker was talking about – with the three identical vases, except one of them is more identical than the others.

Nutscracker
For us to be manipulated like that, we'd have to be wearing helmets.

Organizm(-:
Maybe we are.

Nutscracker
Touch your face with your hands. Can you feel any helmet?

Organism(-:
No, but . . .

Monstradamus

I know what he's going to ask now. He's going to ask whether you can use a helmet to simulate what you feel with your hands.

Organizm(-:

Well that's right. It seems a natural enough question to me.

Nutscracker

If everything is simulated by the helmet, then it's not a helmet or a simulation any more. It's life.

Organizm(-:

Nutscracker, there's one thing you didn't explain. Who switches on all these 'Sticky Eyes' and 'Sunny Kisses'? Surely someone has to control it all?

Nutscracker

Certainly. There's an operator with a special monitor. He sees the Helmholtz as a dot on a radar screen. And the vases would be, say, red rhomboids. There's a manipulation menu on the same screen.

The rest is all just like in Windows — click and drag.

Monstradamus
Click and drag. A great slogan for a double-edged axe.

Organizm(-:
And how can you do it the other way round?

Nutscracker
How do you mean?

Organizm(-:
So the virtual reality helmet is on the operator who controls the manipulation. And this operator some-how makes the others see what he sees.

Nutscracker
How could he make them do that?

Organizm(-:
Hypnosis.

UGLI 666
There you are. I was just waiting for that word.

Nutscracker
I don't know much about hypnosis. But if a hypnotist was powerful enough to make others see what he sees, why would he need a helmet?

Organizm(-:
In order to know what the others have to see.

Monstradamus
You could take it even further. Not just seeing, but actually being there. Asterisk wears a helmet in which he sees a labyrinth. And we're all inside this labyrinth. And he manipulates us.

Nutscracker
You mean we're all inside the Minotaur's head?

Monstradamus
You could say we're in the space that he sees.

Nutscracker
Then where's the Minotaur?

Monstradamus
We have to assume he's in the space that Ariadne
sees in her dreams.

Organizm(-:
End of the line. Remember, Nutcracker, at the very
beginning you asked me 'Where is here exactly?' I
didn't understand your question at first. In the
helmet of horror, that's where.

Nutscracker
That doesn't fit, though. On the one hand, the
Minotaur's manipulating all of us, but on the other
hand, he's got no head . . . But then again, quite
apart from this particular case, I can testify profes-
sionally that's what causes all the problems.

Organizm(-:
Absolutely. This Asterisk has a cheap kettle with a
solar battery in his helmet. How can he decide where

to use 'Sunny Kiss' and where to use 'The Seventh Seal'?

Monstradamus
Automatically. It might all depend on which section of the helmet of horror a bubble of hope happens to burst in.

Organizm(-:
But I'm the one who sees the ray of sunlight or the dove, not Asterisk. I don't understand anything any more. Who's wearing the helmet of horror? Me or the Minotaur?

Nutscracker
The Helmholtz.

Monstradamus
We've been talking about that helmet too long already. It feels like we keep trying it on over and over again. It will attach itself permanently to our heads soon. Let's change the subject.

Organizm(-:

Great idea, let's. I've just had a thought. Has anyone ever wondered why Star Wars has such a strange sequel – instead of filming what came after the third episode, they filmed what came before the first one?

Monstradamus

Why?

Organizm(-:

At the end of the third episode Darth Vader dies, and that's the end of all the Star Wars. There can't be any more, because he's the Minotaur of that world, and that black heap of junk on his head is the helmet of horror. He thinks every one of them: Luke Skywalker, the robots, Chewbacca and all the rest of it. So after he's killed there can't be any continuation.

Monstradamus

But Darth Vader takes his helmet off before he dies. And underneath he has a normal head, only covered in scars.

Organizm(-:
Yes, but it's just a fantasy, after all.

Nutscracker
Yes, Organism. Very profound. And the Iron Mask was another Minotaur. When they handed him over to the Marquis de Sade to be corrupted, the revolution began, because the pain in his xxx made him stop thinking up royalist France.

Romeo-y-Cohiba
Isolde, are you here?

IsoldA
Yes.

Romeo-y-Cohiba
I'm back. What's happening here?

IsoldA
Nothing very interesting. Nutscracker was telling everybody about politics. And I only got back from Versailles just recently.

Monstradamus

Nutcracker, on that business of royalist France. You know, the Marquis turned out not to be so terrible after all.

Romeo-y-Cohiba

It's all very monotonous where I am. Bushes, a bend, bushes, a fork, a bend, on and on for ever. The passage is about six feet wide.

IsoldA

What's that in metres?

Romeo-y-Cohiba

Two. Makes you feel like a rat in a maze. At one point I decided I'd had enough and tried to climb through the hedge. Some chance. There's a barbed-wire mesh fence in the bushes – like the grid of bars in reinforced concrete. And I'd been wondering how they managed to keep the bushes so even!

IsoldA

That labyrinth must lead out into my park. You just

didn't go far enough. We have the same ground under our feet. Beige soil.

Romeo-y-Cohiba

I kept turning to the right. It's funny. A flashback from my childhood. You know the way it is – a memory illuminated by a warm, long-forgotten light that seems to conceal the most important answer of all. Some book of adventure stories you read God only knows how many years ago. Where it said you can get through any labyrinth if you keep turning right all the time. So I decided to try it. Seems it was right – I did find something interesting after all. I saw one of your fountains. It was a long way off, though.

IsoldA

Tell me about it, then.

Romeo-y-Cohiba

At one point in the labyrinth there's a little bench. A perfectly ordinary bench, like they have in parks. I climbed up on it and stood on the back, and my eyes were level with the upper edge of the bushes. On one side I could see a jet of water rising into the air, and on the other, way off in the distance, some kind of dark roof that looked as though it was covered with soot. The roof was hard to make out because it was so far away, and the jet of water was very strange – one jet shooting up into the air, but several of them falling down. Maybe it was an optical illusion.

IsoldA

No, that's right. I know that fountain. It has bronze figures too. There's a snake and a . . . I've forgotten what it's called, like a pig with long spines.

Romeo-y-Cohiba

A porcupine.

IsoldA

Yes, that's it. A porcupine sitting on a bronze tree-stump with water flowing out from it in all directions, as though the beast had suffered bad fright. And the snake is coiled up creeping towards the stump and shooting out a tall jet of water that divides into three branches and falls like rain on the porcupine and everything all around. It's an incredibly beautiful fountain. The first time I saw it there was a little rainbow suspended in the spray of water beside it, and from that moment on I loved it best of all. There are actually three jets of water, but with different pressures. Their nozzles are set close beside each other in the snake's mouth, so it looks as though there's one jet rising into the air and three falling downwards. And I remembered the tattoo on your wrist, the oil and the yacht-club. Does the jet you can see above the bushes divide into three?

Romeo-y-Cohiba
Yes, I think so.

IsoldA
Aren't you absolutely sure?

Romeo-y-Cohiba
I can see a jet of water and the roof of a house when

I climb up on to a bench and stand on the back of it. But it's not possible to stand up there like that for very long, you sway backwards and forwards and then you lose your balance and you have to jump down. That makes it hard to make out the details. But if it is the same fountain you should see my labyrinth when you stand beside it.

IsoldA
There's a tall hedge beside the fountain with the snake and the porcupine and I can't tell what's behind it. It's very long – I walked a little way along it, the bushes fence off a large section of park. I think that must be your enclosure.

Romeo-y-Cohiba
If you've walked along that hedge, at one moment we might only have been ten feet apart. I was beside it too, on my own side. I'm practically certain it was the outside hedge. In the first place, there were two rows of barbed fencing instead of just one in the bushes. And in the second place, there's a spot where you can clearly hear the sound of falling

water. Oh and, by the way, beside the spot with the sound of water there's a long wall protruding from the bushes. It looks like the back of some building and it's painted with pink and gold Cupids blowing seashells like trumpets. Have you got anything like that?

IsoldA

There is a single-storey building to the right of the fountain. It looks like a pavilion for storing garden tools, except that it's very big. Its back section disappears into the high hedge. But I didn't see any Cupids on it.

Romeo-y-Cohiba

Can you get inside?

IsoldA

The door's locked. Is there a door in your wall?

Romeo-y-Cohiba

Yes.

IsoldA
Does it open?

Romeo-y-Cohiba
To be honest I didn't try it. I stood beside it for a while and suddenly I felt terrified, I even got a pounding in my temples. I'm not the timid type at all, but suddenly there it was. For no reason at all. I thought – who knows what's inside there? What if it's the Minotaur?

:-)))

UGLI 666
Nutcracker, do you know any Latin?

Nutscracker
The Senate and People of Rome. P-Q-R-S. No, I'm confusing it with the alphabet. What the Romans had was S-P-Q-R.

Monstradamus
Why are you interested in Latin, Ugly?

UGLI 666

To translate a few words.

Monstradamus

I'll give it a try.

UGLI 666

What's 'aiselceclesia'?

Monstradamus

I don't know.

UGLI 666

And 'ieselceaeclesi'?

Monstradamus

I don't know that either. Are you sure it's Latin?

UGLI 666

What else could it be?

Monstradamus

I can't tell yet. Can you give us the whole phrase?

UGLI 666
It's very long.

Monstradamus
Then a couple of words at least.

UGLI 666
It starts: 'aiselceclesia ieselceaeclesi selceataecles elceatctaecle'.

Monstradamus
Stop, that's enough for now.

UGLI 666
What is it?

Monstradamus
Not so fast. Let me have a think.

Nutscracker
Where's it from, Ugly?

UGLI 666
From a labyrinth.

Nutscracker
Have you got a labyrinth outside your door?

UGLI 666
What else am I supposed to have?

Nutscracker
Catacombs.

Monstradamus
Don't mock, Nutcracker.

UGLI 666
The catacombs were the cradle of the faith. It would have been great reassurance from the Lord.

Nutscracker
She said before she had a hall full of benches. Now all of a sudden there's a labyrinth.

UGLI 666

I wish you'd go back to your bitches, Nutcracker, I really do. Can you make anything of it, Monstradamus?

Monstradamus

Were the words written in a column, one under the other?

UGLI 666

Yes.

Monstradamus

Can you type the one that was in the middle?

UGLI 666

What do you mean? Which one's that?

Monstradamus

The seventh from the top, if that makes it easier.

UGLI 666

Eatcnasanctae.

Nutscracker
Eat NASA. I can't make out any other references there.

Monstradamus
Where did you find it?

UGLI 666
I don't really want to talk about that.

Monstradamus
What if I reproduce the entire inscription, then will you tell me?

UGLI 666
In that case, yes.

Monstradamus
The inscription was this:

```
AISELCECLESIAISELCEAECL
ESISELCEATAECLESELCEAT
CTAECLELCEATCNCTAECLC
EATCEANCTAECEATCNASA
NCTAECEATCNANCTAECLC
EATCNCTAECLELCEATCTAE
CLESELCEATAECLESISELCE
AECLESIAISELCECLESIA
```

UGLI 666

That's right. How did you do that?

Monstradamus

Dominus illuminatio mea.

UGLI 666

But what does it mean?

Monstradamus

The Lord is my light.

UGLI 666

I mean what does my inscription mean?

Monstradamus

Well, what do you think?

UGLI 666

I can't make any sense of it at all. What sense is
there?

Monstradamus

The sense can be very different, depending on where
you found it. So you'll have to be honest about everything.

UGLI 666

All right. Outside my door there really is a hall with
benches. I didn't really look at it properly at first.
But then when I did . . . I'm not even sure whether
you'll believe me or not, Monstradamus.

Monstradamus

I'll give it a try.

UGLI 666

There's a cathedral there. A Gothic cathedral.

Nutscracker

You just said there was a labyrinth.

UGLI 666

That's there too, only inside the cathedral. And in front of the entrance to the labyrinth there's another Latin inscription laid out on the floor:

HVNC MVNDVM TIPICE LABERINTHVS DENOTAT ISTE:
INTRANTI LARGVS, REDEVNTI SED NIMIS ARTVS SIC MVNDO CAPTVS,
VICIORVM MOLLE GRAVATVS VIX VALET AD VITE DOCTRINAM QVISQVE REDIRE.

Monstradamus

The meaning of that is more or less as follows – 'the labyrinth represents the world in which we live, wide at the entrance, but narrow at the exit. He who is ensnared by the joys of this world and is burdened with its sins, may only rediscover the doctrine of life through effort.' Only don't ask me what the doctrine of life is. Was there really a wide entrance and a narrow exit?

UGLI 666

There wasn't any entrance or exit at all in the usual sense. The entire labyrinth was laid out on the floor of the cathedral in light-blue marble. It's just a mosaic.

Nutscracker

Is there such a thing as light-blue marble?

UGLI 666

Yes, there is.

Nutscracker

But what's a labyrinth doing in a cathedral?

UGLI 666

The first canon told me a labyrinth is a part of that church and many others, because it illustrates the full complexity of the Christian path.

Nutscracker

The first canon?

UGLI 666
Yes. But the second canon objected that the Christian
path is as simple and straight as an arrow. And the
twists and turns and dead-ends of the labyrinth
symbolise sin, in which fallen souls wander, hope-
lessly lost. And then the first canon replied that he
had essentially meant the same thing, since sin is a
distortion arising in the straight line of the Christian
path. But no matter how tortuous the path of life
might be, if the person walking it remains within
the bosom of the Church, the simple arithmetic of
good and evil ceases to apply, and the higher mathematics of the spirit comes into play.

Nutscracker
Now we've got a second canon as well.

Monstradamus
And what higher mathematics is that?

UGLI 666
However crooked and tortuous a life may be overall, a
communicant of the Sacred Gifts may regard each

infinitesimally small sector of his path as straight. And if any sector of his path is straight, then it is straight at any moment, and if it is straight at any moment, then it is always straight, and the Lord will not reject his soul. It is as though we grow mathematical wings that lift us up out of the depths of our degradation.

Nutscracker
But who are these canons? You mean you met someone?

UGLI 666
There were two of them. They were praying on bended knees near the altar. I made a noise, they noticed me and came over to help me with explanations and instructions.

Nutscracker
Tell us about them.

UGLI 666
They said that a long time ago, when faith was strong in people's souls, a priest could send a repentant

sinner on a pilgrimage to the Holy Land. In later
times, when faith began to fail . . .

Nutscracker
Not about the instructions, tell us about the canons
themselves. Don't you understand, or what? No one
else here has met anybody.

Monstradamus
What about Ariadne?

Nutscracker
She only dreamed about them. Surely I don't have to
explain the difference?

Monstradamus
Yes, explain it, Nutcracker.

Nutscracker
You don't understand the difference between a dream
and reality?

Monstradamus

I don't understand what the difference is between the two stories.

Nutscracker

The difference is one's about a dream and one's about reality.

Monstradamus

But all I can see are letters on a screen.

Nutscracker

Not again. You've worn me out. Ugly, are you there?

UGLI 666

Yes.

Nutscracker

These canons, what did they look like?

UGLI 666

Medium height. In threadbare cassocks, with old-fashioned, wide-brimmed cardinal's hats on their heads. The canons explained that the hats once belonged to holy prelates and they helped to calm the passions. The second canon had the brim of his hat bent upwards at one side, like a duellist. It reminded me of Aramis from 'The Three Musketeers', the one who was an ordinary sinner at first, and then became a general of the order of Jesuits.

Monstradamus
Sounds like the two dwarves that Ariadne saw at the very beginning.

Nutscracker
That's what I thought too. But those were dwarves, and these two are medium height.

Monstradamus
Ugly, what height are you?

UGLI 666
That has nothing to do with anything.

Nutscracker

Forget it. Let's move on. Ugly, did you see their faces?

UGLI 666

No. They stood with their heads bowed, as befits monks and spiritual people, and the brims of their hats hid their features completely.

Nutscracker

And what were their voices like?

UGLI 666

Humble and sincere.

Nutscracker

What did they say?

UGLI 666

I started telling you that, but you interrupted. They said that in the glorious times of the Holy Crusades, especially after the victory of Gottfried of Bouillon, pilgrims journeyed on foot to the grave of our Lord to repent. Later, when faith grew weaker and the human spirit no longer possessed the strength for such great effort, the site of pilgrimage was relocated to monasteries and abbeys, where people went to pay homage to the local saint. When people's piety became too weak even for that, they were instructed to walk The League to do penance.

Nutscracker
The League?

UGLI 666
Yes. It's the old name for the church labyrinth. That's approximately how long it was. Although the one I was facing was a lot shorter. You were supposed to walk through these labyrinths on your knees. And for the time of ultimate decline that will come just before the end of the world, labyrinths on walls were prepared, really small ones that people go through by tracing the way with their finger. They are for those who are only willing to spend a very small amount of time on their souls. But there are labyrinths that are quite the opposite, endlessly long ones in which you can repent eternally. For instance

in the Church of Sta. Maria-di-Trastavera in Rome. The first canon showed me a plan of it.

Monstradamus
He prepared well for the conversation.

UGLI 666
He didn't prepare for it. The plans of the labyrinths were on the columns and walls of the cathedral. In fact, everything there was covered with them. The one that's in Sta. Maria-di-Trastavera consists of a large number of circles set inside each other. It looks like a target for shooting practice. It's the most mystical of all the labyrinths.

Monstradamus
The most mystical one is mine; please enter that in the minutes.

UGLI 666
The second canon explained that the meaning of these circles is that it's no more possible for the soul to approach the Lord through its own desire than for

the moon suddenly to decide to fly closer to the earth. The soul will remain eternally on the plane to which the Lord has sent it, and it will only be able to approach Him through His mercy, and not of its own will. And His mercy is expressed in the existence of the Church. It's the Church that lends us those mathematical wings we were talking about. Without them we can only circle around Him like the planets. Sin is the centrifugal force that pulls us away from Him. But God's love is like the force of gravity, because it draws us to Him. The soul dwells in this world below because these forces balance each other.

Nutscracker
So the Lord loves sinners more then?

UGLI 666
Why?

Nutscracker
They have more sins, so their centrifugal force is stronger. For them to stay in orbit, the force of God's love has to increase to balance it.

UGLI 666

But it happens in families too, that the best-loved children are the naughtiest.

Nutscracker

Then that means, if you want the Lord to love you, pull as many dirty tricks as you can?

UGLI 666

Yes it does, according to logic. But I'm not really sure that's what the Lord is actually guided by.

Nutscracker

Okay, we'll check that one out. What happened next?

UGLI 666

Next? The second canon folded his arms and fell silent and withdrew humbly into the shadow. I began walking around the cathedral arm-in-arm with the first one, examining the plans of the various spiritual labyrinths, while the canon quietly explained their function and symbolic meaning to me. I thought the labyrinth from Poitiers Cathedral was particularly beautiful. It's shaped like a tree with a spreading crown and arranged so that the same threshold serves as its entrance and its exit. It works out like that because the path only divides in two once, at the very centre, and its two halves twist and turn to form the right and left parts of the tree's crown. The canon said it was the Tree of Life, and the meaning of the labyrinth was that we enter life and leave it through the same door, naked and taking nothing with us.

Nutscracker
And where's that inscription with the secret message from, the one you asked us to translate?

UGLI 666
From an ancient basilica in Algeria.

Monstradamus
Does it have a labyrinth too?

UGLI 666
Yes. It surrounds a central square containing the holy inscription. The canon told me to copy it out and

assured me there was a secret in the inscription. He said I would only be able to read it when I had the key. In exactly the same way, he said, I would not be able to understand the predestined purpose of people and things in this world until the moment when the wisdom that comes with true faith opened my eyes to the transcendental meaning of creation. And the key to that wisdom was the same as the key to the inscription. He also told me not to be seduced by the empty talk about Theseus, which he knows all about. In time, he said, I would see for myself that the true Theseus is the One whom he serves. And that's all. Is Monstradamus still there?

Nutscracker
Later. Go on with your story.

UGLI 666
I'm not going to tell you any more until he translates for me.

Nutscracker
Monster, are you there? Translate for her, please.

Monstradamus

The whole point is in the way the letters are arranged. In French it's called a *jeu-de-lettres*.

UGLI 666

But do you have the key to the inscription the canon was talking about?

Monstradamus

Of course.

UGLI 666

What is it?

Monstradamus

It's a cross.

UGLI 666

My Lord! Thy will be done!

Monstradamus

Yes. You have to start from the very centre. Find the letter S there and trace a cross through it. If you read the text in any direction of the cross and then along any line from it at right angles, you get SANCTA ECLESIA, which means 'the holy church', with one mistake.

UGLI 666
Are you saying the inscription was made with a spelling mistake? Or does the inscription refer to a mistake made by the holy church?

Monstradamus
What I'm saying is there should be two C's in the word for church – ecclesia. But in olden times they might have thought that was excessive.

Nutscracker
Then what happened, Ugly?

UGLI 666
Wait a moment. Let me see if it works with the letters. It really does. How profound! Now I understand what the canon was trying to say, Monstradamus. This world will remain a meaning-

less conglomeration of absurdities and riddles, where we continue to wander aimlessly about in the dark, until we accept the teachings of the Holy Church. But as soon as that happens, the holy cross will shine out at the centre of life's labyrinth, and the fullness of the purpose concealed in all things will instantly be revealed! The world will be miraculously transformed, the harmonious scheme of things will emerge from the chaos and insanity, and whichever way we direct our gaze, we shall see Hosannah to the Lord on every side! Is that right, Monstradamus?

Monstradamus
But of course. And we shall hear the radiance of his glory.

Nutscracker
Amen. So what happened next?

UGLI 666
The canon led me over to the labyrinth laid out on the floor and said 'My daughter, the One whom

— 149 —

I serve wishes you to walk The League and repent.'
I went down on my knees and set off. The canon
said that while walking through a labyrinth like
that the correct thing to do is to meditate intensely
on everything that you have done in your life. I
didn't have to try very hard. I only had to glance
at the grid by the altar for pictures of my childhood to start floating past my inner eye like
coloured balloons, magically transforming what I
saw around me. With every new second I was
immersed deeper and deeper into the past. The
majestic columns soaring upwards to meet
the distant vaults took on the appearance of the
lime trees in the park in xxx where I spent the first
few years of my life. It's not surprising – in those
distant days the trees were every bit as huge in
relation to me as those columns are now. The
images of the saints watching me from niches in
the walls had the faces of grown-ups from my
childhood. I sensed that some of them were strict
and others were indulgent, but they all loved me
equally, even though they knew absolutely everything about me. Then the path turned a corner and

I began walking, or rather crawling, in a different direction; now I remembered the time of my youth. The stone boatman decorating the preacher's pulpit came to life and sailed across the waters of my memory, transformed into the only friend of my life's brief springtime. He looked exactly as he did on the lake in xxx, where we swore to love each other forever. A new turn, and sin had swept him into oblivion – I no longer knew him and did not wish to know him. Yet another turn and the time of maturity had arrived. My stockings were worn into holes, my knees were scratched, but I didn't feel any pain – tears of repentance and hope were flowing down my cheeks. And the Lord sent me word, yes He did! A little miracle occurred – I don't know how it happened that in my blindness I only realised it afterwards, when I came back to my cell. I mean my room. As I circled through the labyrinth, no matter which way I turned within it, I could always see the crucifixion with a ray of sunlight falling on it through a stained-glass window, suffusing it with ruby, emerald and sapphire light! And that unearthly radiance made my heart feel so happy, so bright and calm that I wanted to cry and sing, cry and sing . . .

Nutscracker
And?

UGLI 666
Cry and sing.

Nutscracker
And is that it?

UGLI 666
Yes, that's more or less everything. When I'd crawled all the way through the labyrinth, the canons were no longer anywhere to be seen. I walked out of the cathedral and found myself in my room.

Nutscracker
And can you go back into the cathedral now?

UGLI 666
Its door is locked now.

Nutscracker

When did they find time to lock it?

UGLI 666

I don't know.

Nutscracker

And are you sure you didn't just dream it all, like Ariadne?

UGLI 666

Yes, I'm sure. The canon gave me a rosary and I'm holding it in my hand. I'm going to take a rest now.

Monstradamus

Yes, Ugly, take a rest. After all you've been through it will do you good.

Nutscracker

An interesting crossword puzzle. But from a mystical point of view, how do you explain that at the very centre of the labyrinth of life there lies the letter 'S'?

Monstradamus
That ought to be clear enough to you of all people,
Nutcracker.

Nut$cracker
Why?

Monstradamus
You have the same letter at your centre too. And just
at the moment it's looking really lovely.

Nutscracker
Where? Oh, that. That's the moderators taking the
piss again. If that's what you had in mind, I can tell
you the pay for my job is so low it's an insult.

Romeo-y-Cohiba
Isolde, are you back yet?

Monstradamus
Hi there, Romeo.

Romeo-y-Cohiba
Are you IsoldA then?

Nutscracker
Cohiba's in a bad mood today.

Monstradamus
I liked the phrase 'With every new second I was immersed deeper and deeper into the past.'

Nutscracker
Yes, I noticed that too.

Monstradamus
Pure poetry. With every new day we slide deeper and deeper into the past. We disappear into it, like a diver sinking under the water in a slow-motion sequence. What is the difference between an old man and a young man if you put them side by side?

Nutscracker
One of them is old and one of them is young.

Monstradamus

Yes, but what does that mean? That there is only a tiny little piece of the old man left in our dimension – he is almost completely submerged in Lethe's waters of oblivion. But the young man is still all here – he has just barely touched the surface of the water. Isn't that it?

Nutscracker

I don't know. The way things are these days, they could both go down together at any moment. And the size of the pieces would depend less on their age than the force of the blast.

Monstradamus

That's also true.

Nutscracker

And, as for that phrase you liked, I think Ugly was thinking of the helmet of horror. The future is produced from the past, so the further we go into the future, the more past is required to produce it. You know, the closer you build to the stars, the deeper the pit you dig the soil out of . . .

Romeo-y-Cohiba
Isolde, are you there? Isolde!

Nutscracker
And, to complete the picture, you could say the bubbles of the past were bursting in a helmet that was running 'Sticky Eye' and 'Sunny Kiss' simultaneously.

UGLI 666
What?

Monstradamus
Are you still here, Ugly? Take no notice, he's joking.

UGLI 666
I should never have told you.

Monstradamus
Don't be offended, Ugly.

UGLI 666
I'm never going to tell you anything again.

Monstradamus
Say you're sorry, Nutcracker.

Nutscracker
For what?

Monstradamus
Please, say you're sorry.

Nutscracker
All right. I'm sorry, Ugly.

UGLI 666
God will forgive you.

IsoldA
Romeo, where are you? I'm back.

Romeo-y-Cohiba
I was starting to get worried. Tell me what happened.

IsoldA
You first.

Romeo-y-Cohiba
All right. I would have reached the pavilion quickly,
because last time I marked which way to go at the
forks in the path. But I met someone really terrifying on the way.

IsoldA
You too?

Romeo-y-Cohiba
What happened? Are you all right?

Isolde
Yes, everything's fine. Go on.

Romeo-y-Cohiba
When I got past the bench where I can see the roof
and the fountain, I suddenly sensed a movement
behind me. And when I turned round I saw something absolutely incredible. Just imagine it, a long

narrow corridor between the bushes. And coming towards me along it on roller skates was . . . I don't even know if it was a man or not. He was immensely tall, wearing a sombrero hat and an ice-hockey goal-keeper's mask made of white plastic. And there were two smaller figures on roller skates behind him. I could hardly see them, because he took up the entire passage. He was wearing a goalkeeper's uniform too – an immense blue sweatshirt with the number '35' and the words 'CHICAGO BULLS'. Or at least, that's what I thought at first. But when he got closer, I could see the number was actually totally weird: '–3.5%', and the word 'BULLS' was really 'BEARS'. It was just that the minus sign and the percentage sign were the same colour as the sweatshirt and I hadn't spotted them from the distance. And he was hold-ing a double hockey-stick.

IsoldA
How do you mean?

Romeo-y-Cohiba
You've seen a goalkeeper's stick, haven't you? Now

imagine it has two blades curving in opposite directions. Of course, you couldn't possibly play with one like that.

IsoldA
And what happened when he reached you?

Romeo-y-Cohiba
He didn't get that far. When he was only ten feet away, he turned a corner and disappeared into a side passage. And the others darted in there after him as well.

IsoldA
Who was it following him?

Romeo-y-Cohiba
It was two dwarves. They were on roller skates too, and wearing sombreros. I couldn't see their faces, they had their heads lowered so the wind wouldn't blow their hats off. And they were holding up the hem at the back of his sweatshirt, like ladies in waiting.

IsoldA

Was that all?

Romeo-y-Cohiba

Fortunately, yes. Who did you meet?

IsoldA

It was at the corner of one of the alleys. I heard the sound of a guitar string behind me. When I turned round, about twenty metres away from me I saw an immensely tall man standing beside a fountain. He was dressed all in black and gold like an eighteenth-century gallant, and he was hiding his face behind a mask in the form of a golden sun that he was holding on a stick. There were two dwarves dressed up in red velvet standing beside him, holding old pot-bellied guitars. They strummed a few soft chords, then the giant turned his mask slightly and the sun glinted on it so brightly I was dazzled and I screwed up my eyes. And when I opened them again there was no one beside the fountain any more. I didn't even have time to be scared and I thought I must have had a hallucination after everything I'd been hearing. But now I don't know what to think. You go on.

Romeo-y-Cohiba

Well, I decided that if the giant had wanted to kill me he would have done it already. So I carried on as though nothing had happened. I didn't meet anyone else on the way. The door in the wall of the pavilion was open. And behind it there was a winding corridor. Naturally, there was no light. The floorboards squeaked horribly, as if every one of them had three mice sitting under it. It was absolutely terrifying. There were doors in the walls and more doors behind them. I began groping my way at random through the musty, squeaking darkness and became disorientated straightaway. I was overcome by apathy. I wanted to drop down on the floor, close my eyes and forget about absolutely everything. Probably that's what I would have done, but then one of the doors led me out into a large room where there was a light on. It was deserted and dusty, with no windows and divided in half by a set of steel bars so thick they could have kept out an elephant. There was no furniture at all, if you didn't count several pictures turned around so that the images faced the wall. I thought it was probably so they wouldn't get dusty – clever and very simple, no need for any glass. Hanging on the door, which closed behind my back, was a plaque that said 'Silence!' And beyond the bars was a fresco with a portrait of the most beautiful girl I've ever seen. Right across the whole wall.

IsoldA
A girl right across the whole wall?

Romeo-y-Cohiba
No, the fresco. Some kind of garden full of wonderful plants and birds. And the girl was at the very centre, life-size. Absolutely naked, but it suited her really well. She had green hair that looked like grass, fluttering in the painted breeze. And green eyelashes too. She was lying in a mother-of-pearl shell, barely concealing the lower part of her belly with a bouquet of flowers. There was one strange thing, though – the edge of the shell above her head was covered with projections that looked like horns. And there were

black rubber handles attached to them. That is, the projections were painted, but the handles were real, like in a bus. I touched them and I could tell it really was possible to hold on to them. But I couldn't understand what for.

IsoldA

How could you touch them? You said there were bars between the door and the fresco.

Romeo-y-Cohiba

That's right. But it was easy enough to slip between the bars. So that's what I did. They probably weren't meant to keep out people.

IsoldA

Describe this girl.

Romeo-y-Cohiba

I suppose she was about eighteen, but she didn't look any older than fourteen. I'd describe her pose as brazen, but entirely natural. What I mean is, the pose would have been absolutely brazen, if she'd been lying there like that, knowing that she was being watched. But if she lay around like that at home, especially if it was hot, then of course, there wouldn't be anything brazen about it. But on the other hand, she was looking straight out of the picture at the spectator, which in this case meant straight at me. She had her eyes half-closed, as though she could see me and was taunting me, and she was smiling. And her eyes were as green as could be. I began to understand what the artist was trying to say. Either she'd posed like that knowing she was being watched, which meant she was absolutely shameless, which I didn't want to believe. Or she'd been lying like that because she thought there was no one around, and she was smiling at the spectator simply out of inertia, because she'd only just noticed him. In that case the artist was a real genius, because he'd caught the precise moment when her brain had already given the command to scream, but the command still hadn't reached the muscles of her throat. In that case, for as long as I carried on examining her, I was free of shame myself, so free in fact that it was actually arousing. In a word, genuine art. An absolutely enigmatic masterpiece. But I didn't have time to study her properly, because the bouquet she was using to conceal the lower part of her belly trembled and started sliding downwards. And it wasn't just the lower part of her belly she'd been hiding, but the lowest part of all, so low you can't get any lower, only higher . . .

IsoldA
All right, Romeo, I get the idea.

Romeo-y-Cohiba
There must have been some kind of mechanism in the wall. The arm that was holding the bouquet began turning from the elbow, like the hand of a clock. But I didn't get a chance to see what was behind the bouquet, because the light began to fade and soon it was completely dark. I went up to the wall and began feeling it with my hands. Where the bouquet had been quite a big gap had appeared. I put my hand into it carefully and suddenly felt something soft and alive that jerked away from me. I think it was another hand. I cried out in surprise and

suddenly there was a spray of something acrid from the ceiling, like tear gas. I jumped back. The light started coming on. When it was bright enough to see, the bouquet was already back in place. My eyes were stinging really badly and I ran out of the room like it was a gas chamber.

IsoldA
Do your eyes still hurt?

Romeo-y-Cohiba
Not any more.

IsoldA
Now I see.

Romeo-y-Cohiba
What do you see, Isolde?

IsoldA
It seems I discovered the same amusement arcade from the other side. After the giant with the sun-mask disappeared, I went to the pavilion. The door was

locked. And the windows too. I broke a window, lifted the latch and opened it. Behind the first door was the beginning of a dark, winding corridor like the one you told me about. From there I found my way into a large room with a light and no windows, just like you did. Instead of pictures it had mirrors painted over with white paint. Standing in the middle of the room was an absolutely huge steel ring as tall as the ceiling, with nylon mesh attached all around its edge – it hung down from the ring and trailed across the floor like a seine net. On the door there was a plaque about keeping silent, just like on yours. And on the wall behind the ring there was a mural, only it was very different from yours. It was a picture of something like the Grand Canyon. Through the mist I could make out the desert floor far below me. And on the edge of the red cliff, right up in front of the spectator's eyes, there was a car with a cloud of painted dust settling around it. It all looked just as though the car had braked after a steep turn and stopped at the very last moment, with its wheels hanging over the edge of the precipice. It was a Rolls-Royce jeep, in perfect profile, like a photo in an advert.

Romeo-y-Cohiba
Are you sure it was a Rolls-Royce?

IsoldA
Of course. It had the initials 'RR' and a little Oscar with wings on the radiator, like they all have.

Romeo-y-Cohiba
Then it wasn't a jeep. Rolls-Royce don't make jeeps.

IsoldA
Romeo, I can tell my SUV from my elbow. I even saw the name of the model – 'Full Drive Shadow' I think it was. That's the whole point. It was an artist's fantasy, but it was so convincing I could see straight away that if Rolls-Royce decided to make an SUV they'd have to make the car that was painted there; circumstances would simply force them to do it. The jeep was made of gold and steel, like an exquisite watch. To say it looked impressive gives you no idea. If the space shuttle and the most expensive diamond necklace in the world could together produce a son, then it would probably look just like that when it

grew up. In front of the jeep was a platform with steps. I mean the platform wasn't in the picture, it was on the floor of the room, real, made of wooden boards. And the jeep's windows were real too, tinted glass that looked black and there were skis and a surf-board on its roof.

Romeo-y-Cohiba
Real ones?

IsoldA
The skis and the board were painted. But the rack they were attached to, or that they looked as if they were attached to in the painting, was real, made of steel and gold.

Romeo-y-Cohiba
What kind of rack?

IsoldA
I don't know what its proper name is – the kind they make so you can tie on what you carry on the roof. There were loops of black leather hanging from it,

like the ones used for doing gymnastics; they were real as well. And, apart from that, the door handles and the hub-caps were real – and they were made of steel and gold too.

Romeo-y-Cohiba
Did you try opening the door?

IsoldA
I told you, there weren't any doors, only handles. But I didn't even get a chance to touch them. The moment I took a couple of steps towards the jeep, its window began slowly winding down. Some kind of mechanism must have switched on. I really wanted to find out what was behind the glass, but the light began to fade, and a few seconds later it was dark. Exactly the same thing as happened to you, in fact. I climbed up on the platform and touched the wall where the window of the jeep had been. There was a gap there now. I ran my hand round its edge. It really felt like a car window. But the window hadn't opened all the way and the gap wasn't big enough to climb through the wall. There was a slight draught

from the window, as if there was an air-conditioner working inside. And I thought I caught a faint glimpse of light. I leaned down to look inside, but as soon as my face was level with the opening something bumped against my cheek and I heard a terrible howl. I leapt back, lost my balance and fell off the platform on to the floor. The light came on – dim at first, then brighter and brighter, like in the cinema after a film. By the time it got really light, the jeep's window was already closed again. I went back out through the corridor into the open air and came back here. I was shaking all over at first, but I started feeling better on the way. It's funny to think about it now.

Romeo-y-Cohiba
Well, I've learned one lesson. Nice and easy does it.

IsoldA
Yes. Especially in your RR SUV.

Romeo-y-Cohiba
It's your RR SUV.

IsoldA
Why?

Romeo-y-Cohiba
It's on your side!

IsoldA
But you're the one inside it. That means it's yours.

Romeo-y-Cohiba
How can it be mine if I can't see it?

IsoldA
And how can it be mine if I can't even get into it?
Apart from sticking my head in the window.

Romeo-y-Cohiba
Let's say it's ours then. Then we can't be wrong.

IsoldA
Agreed.

Romeo-y-Cohiba

Isolde . . . I want to tell you something. It will probably sound stupid, but I want you to hear it anyway.
Whatever I'm thinking about, I always come back to
you. As if all the thoughts that aren't connected with
you are heavy weights and as soon as my mind tries
to deal with them, the effort becomes too much. But
everything to do with you is light and happy, like
the bubbles in champagne. I just want to go on and
on thinking about it.

IsoldA

Yes, Romeo, that really did sound stupid. But I could
say the same thing to you.

Romeo-y-Cohiba

Why don't we meet again at the same place? Say tomorrow afternoon? Calmly, without any fuss. Or any noise.

IsoldA

But what if we're being followed? I mean there,
inside.

Romeo-y-Cohiba

The light goes out when the window opens.

IsoldA

Haven't you ever heard of infra-red cameras? They could do more than just watch us. They could shoot an entire movie.

Romeo-y-Cohiba

Then who would they show it to?

IsoldA

Your wife, for instance. Or Ariadne in a dream.

Romeo-y-Cohiba

I haven't got a wife. And I couldn't give a damn for Ariadne and her dreams. If we start worrying about spies, pretty soon the world will be full of them.

IsoldA

You're right. The only way to be alone is to behave as though we are already alone.

Romeo-y-Cohiba
So it's a date then?

IsoldA
Tomorrow at three, Romeo. I date your car.

Romeo-y-Cohiba
Our car. My green-eyed Lolita. My lovely Mona Lita.

IsoldA
And now to sleep, Cohiba. Be seeing you.

Nutscracker
Be seeing you, be seeing you. Monster, are you there?

Monstradamus
Yes. Where else could I be?

Nutscracker
Well, what do you make of that?

Monstradamus
No doubt our master shed a great big sentimental

tear. The twilight of Ancient Greek thought in a nutshell. Zeno's paradoxes. Achilles can't go riding in his big beautiful car. Because when he's riding in it, he can't see it. The passers-by can see it, so they're the ones riding in it. And Achilles only imagines he's driving it, but in actual fact it's driving him.

Nutscracker
I feel a bit jealous. How about you?

Monstradamus
Not particularly. I don't like jeeps. You're too high above the road when you sit in them. And anyway an RR SUV is a bit OTT. Cohiba ought to have an Alfa Romeo.

Nutscracker
I don't mean the car. Alfa Romeo, Beta Romeo – all that sounds like the stud ranking in a herd of chimpanzees to me. I mean the feelings.

Monstradamus
But you have them too. They have love, you have

envy. As comrade Ariadne teaches us, these are merely different states assumed by past within the helmet of horror.

Nutscracker
And on that optimistic note . . .

Monstradamus
Yes indeed. Good night.

:-))))

Organizm(-:
Who wants to chat?

Ariadne
I do.

Nutscracker
And I do.

Monstradamus
And I do I suppose.

Organizm(-:

An interesting team. Monstradamus, Ariadne, me and Nutcracker. Has anyone noticed that the four of us have something in common?

Nutscracker

It would be hard not to notice. We all use toilet paper with a little star on it.

Monstradamus

And we share a great passion for life.

Organizm(-:

That's not all, though.

Nutscracker

We've all been fed garbage just recently as well. Did everyone get that putrid lasagne yesterday? And how did you like today's vegetarian beefsteak, rare and bloody?

Organizm(-:

That's not it either.

Monstradamus
I know what he means. None of us has said anything about our labyrinths.

Ariadne
Really? It's just that no one's asked me.

Nutscracker
And are you willing to tell us?

Ariadne
Of course.

Nutscracker
So what have you got outside your door?

Ariadne
A bedroom.

Nutscracker
What, just an ordinary bedroom?

Ariadne

No, not ordinary. If you ever leaf through those fashionable journals with all the chic interiors, you might have seen something of the kind. It's a large room, and the bed takes up at least half of it. The mattress is so wonderful I don't even know how to describe it. I should write more poems. When you lie down on it, it feels like you're parachuting through the air, soaring along the pillows, the blankets and the sheets – everything is absolutely the very best. And there's an air conditioner with heaps of different operating modes. You can set it so that a fresh breeze blows through the room as though it's coming straight off the sea. And there are thick curtains on the window that . . .

Nutscracker

You've got a window? What does it look out on?

Ariadne

I don't know. There's some kind of garden, and the branches of trees. I can't see anything else.

Nutscracker
Have you tried opening it?

Ariadne
The window doesn't open. What else now? There's a really elegant wall-lamp above the bed and a night-lamp in the corner. There's a mini-bar too, only there aren't any drinks in it, nothing but little boxes of sleeping pills. There are lots and lots of them, all beautiful kinds of colours, and inside each one there are instructions on how many pills you can take at once, which ones you can take with others, which ones you can't, and so on. Only I don't need any sleeping pills. I only have to lie down on the bed, and I'm gone. I just fly away.

Nutscracker
And is that all there is?

Ariadne
When I leave the bedroom for a long time – say an hour or more – someone changes the sheets and makes the bed. But I haven't met anyone, not even

once. And there aren't any other doors in the bedroom, there's only one way in.

Nutscracker
How do you explain that?

Ariadne
I don't try. It's less scary that way.

Nutscracker
A labyrinth like that could give you bedsores, Ariadne.

Ariadne
You weren't listening to what I said, Nutcracker. The mattress I have is so wonderful I can't even feel it. What bedsores? An angel could sleep on it without even creasing its wings.

Monstradamus
That's an interesting subject. How angels sleep.

Ariadne
Probably like bats, on a coral perch. And they have
special gold hooks on their slippers.

Monstradamus
Perhaps. Only they hang head-up, because they aren't
attracted by the earth's gravity, only by the love of the
Lord. Like Ugly said. Angels are non-material beings.

Organizm(-:
Then how did they manage to choose wives for themselves from among the daughters of man and beget
children?

Nutscracker
Ugly probably knows about that. Or she can check
with some of her friends. Ugly, are you there?

Monstradamus
By the way, on the subject of checking with your
friends. Ariadne, you said we could ask you questions
about the helmet of horror in case you have another
dream about our management.

Ariadne

Of course.

Monstradamus

I have three. Firstly, I really would like to know how everything else can be manufactured out of nothing. And secondly, how the helmet of horror can be located inside one of its own parts, and does that mean that inside one helmet there is a second one, and inside the second a third one, and so on to infinity in both directions? And the final question is – exactly how does the separator labyrinth work?

Ariadne

All right, I'll ask.

Nutscracker

And at the same time ask them to say something about the occipital braid. So far we don't know a single thing about it.

Organizm(-:
I have a question – why is the helmet of horror called
that?

Ariadne
All right. I'll be going then.

Monstradamus
Just like that?

Ariadne
I'll forget the questions later.

Nutscracker
Go on then. And we'll carry on here. What was that
you said about your labyrinth. Monster?

Monstradamus
When was that?

Nutscracker
When Ugly was telling us about the cathedral. They
showed her something like a target and said it was

the most mystical labyrinth there could possibly be. And you claimed the most mystical one was yours. I'm curious about what it is.

Monstradamus
I think I really ought to take those words back. The most mystical one is probably Sartrik's. Sartrik, are you there?

Nutscracker
He must be busy with his booze now.

Monstradamus
Then tell me about your labyrinth. Or Organism can tell us about his.

Organizm(-:
I haven't got anything interesting. Just a screen-saver.

Monstradamus
What?

Organizm(-:
In Windows there's a screen-saver called 'maze'. And I've got a model of it here. Built out of planks instead of pixels. It's the only time I can ever recall software being turned into hardware.

Monstradamus
Did anyone understand that?

Nutscracker
I know what he's talking about. It's a kind of program.

Monstradamus
And it switches off the screen?

Nutscracker
Just the opposite, it switches it on to full power.

Monstradamus
Then why's it called a screen-saviour? What kind of salvation is that?

Nutscracker

Ugly can ask her canons about that. They know all about saviours and salvation.

UGLI 666

If that is a blasphemous insult to the Saviour, He'll forgive you for it, you sinful simpleton. But I advise you to leave the Holy Spirit alone.

Nutscracker

Ah, you're back. Am I correct in suspecting your saviour also doubles up as the creator?

UGLI 666

That's right.

Nutscracker

Do you know who he reminds me of? A spiteful little sorcerer who gets the urge to torture a kitten. So he goes down into a deep, dark cellar, moulds a kitten out of clay, brings it to life and then – whack! – he smashes its head against the corner of the wall. And he does that every weekend, a hundred times or more.

And to make sure no miaowing is ever heard from the cellar, our sorcerer teaches the kittens to think stoically – I came from the dust and to the dust I return. And he forces them to pray to him for the few seconds of their existence.

Monstradamus
God only knows what goes on inside that head of yours, Nutcracker.

UGLI 666
Not God, the devil. That's already a blasphemy against the Holy Ghost, take care Nutcracker. The Lord does not force us to pray to him. We choose our own path, because he created us with free will.

Nutscracker
Don't make me laugh, Ugly. Free will. Life's like falling off a roof. Can you stop on the way? No. Can you turn back? No. Can you fly off sideways? Only in an advertisement for underpants specially made for jumping off roofs. All free will means is you can choose whether to fart in mid-flight or wait till you

hit the ground. And that's what all the philosophers argue about.

UGLI 666
Nutcracker, you're always trying to turn any conversation into a farting match. I must say sometimes you manage it.

Monstradamus
Stop it will you, you're like little children. Let's just drop it. Why don't you tell us about this screensaver, Organism?

Organizm(-:
It's a standard program. If you don't touch the keyboard for a few minutes, a labyrinth with red-brick walls appears on the screen, with a camera moving through it. It has all sorts of bells and whistles, like stones that turn everything upside down when you bump into them. The ceiling becomes the floor, the floor becomes the ceiling, and the camera starts turning in the opposite direction at the forks in the path. There's a big rat in the labyrinth too.

I've actually got two screen-savers like that. The first one appears on the screen when I forget about you lot for a long time. And the second is right outside my door, constructed fairly accurately out of plywood and planks. It even has a rat in it – a kind of little mat with a plush face and paws sewn on to it. Sometimes the rat is lying in the passage. Sometimes it's glued to the ceiling. There are tumble-stones too, blocks of grey plastic. Only they don't turn anything upside down. If you touch one of them, the maze freezes.

Nutscracker
What do you mean, it freezes?

Organizm(-:
That's what I call it, like a computer program. What happens is, the light goes out and a panel lights up above the tumble-stone: 'This program has performed an illegal operation and will be shut down. If the problem persists, contact the program vendor.'

Nutscracker
Then what happens?

Organizm(-:
I have to go home in the dark. And that's a bit of a drag, because the voices start to get on my nerves.

Nutscracker
What voices?

Organizm(-:
All kinds. Quiet and loud. Women, men, even children. Sometimes far away. Sometimes close up.

Nutscracker
So what do these voices say?

Organizm(-:
Always the same thing: 'I am the vendor, I am the vendor. What will you do? What can you do?'

Nutscracker
Yes, you've been screwed all right. And doesn't Bull Gates ever get in touch?

Organizm(-:
No, he doesn't.

Nutscracker
Maybe he does, but you just don't understand. Maybe the Minotaur's actually the dead rat on the ceiling.

Organizm(-:
Maybe. Anyway, if you don't touch these stones, and avoid doing a couple of other things, you can walk right round the labyrinth without any bother. And then you realise fairly quickly it's not a real labyrinth at all, just a big concrete cellar with plywood partitions.

Nutscracker
Have you tried breaking down the partitions?

Organizm(-:
If you shift them even slightly, the whole thing freezes instantly. Then you have to find your way out in the dark and listen to those voices. It's better not to touch anything.

Nutscracker
Have you reached the centre then?

Organizm(-:
Yes, I have.

Nutscracker
And what's in it?

Organizm(-:
A little room with the words 'Open GL' on the wall. The real screen-saver has the same words, but they hang in the air there, and here they're daubed on the plywood in gloss paint. What does that mean, anyway?

Nutscracker
Do you know, Monster?

Monstradamus
Open General License. Or maybe Open Great
Labyrinth.

Nutscracker
So there's nothing but those words in the central
room, Organism, is that right?

Organizm(-:
There's a chair as well, with a mirror in front of it.

Nutscracker
I can guess. Tarkovsky's Mirror.

Organizm(-:
I sat there for ages and ages. I had the feeling I
was about to understand the most important thing
of all at any moment. But I didn't understand a
thing.

Monstradamus
That's always the way.

Organizm(-:
What do you mean? Always the way when you sit looking into a mirror for a long time?

Monstradamus
Always the way when you feel you're just about to understand something important. It's like the whistle of a bullet or the roar of an aeroplane. If you can hear them, it means they're already zooming past you.

Nutscracker
Organism, why are you so sure the centre of the labyrinth is where the mirror and the chair are?

Organizm(-:
Because of the mirror and the chair. What else would they be doing there?

Monstradamus
That seems pretty obvious.

Nutscracker

So what have you got, Monster? I'm dying of
curiosity.

Monstradamus

You go first, we agreed.

Nutscracker

Okay. I'll tell you what I've got. It's a bit like a TV
editing room. Professional equipment – a Betacam
VCR, a special monitor, all sorts of mixers for func-
tions I don't really understand. The whole works.
There's a weird-looking poster hanging on the wall,
a picture of a dog in an empty white room. On the
wall in front of the dog there's something like a
distribution board with a few little lamps screwed
into it. Two of them are lit up – a red one on the
left and a blue one on the right. And below the lamps
there's a bell, surrounded by drawings of sound
waves – it's obviously ringing. There's an electrode
inserted into the dog's head, with wires leading from
it to the distribution board. And there's a cut on its
belly stuck together with sticking plaster and a

rubber tube leading down out of it into a glass flask standing on the floor. The dog's right paw is raised, its tongue is hanging out, its ears are pricked up and its eyes are full of love. The text underneath it reads: 'Put it there, bro!' The first time I saw it I just froze. I wondered how the moderators could have found out. It was only afterwards I remembered I told you all about 'Pavlov's Bitch'. Standing under the poster there's a safe full of Betacam tapes with episodes of 'The Hornists of Plenitude' – that's a kind of chic international TV programme, it has these interesting titles, with the globe flanked by two bugles. The tapes all contain pretty much the same thing: a television address by someone putting himself forward for the job of Theseus. In most cases the candidate is a middle-aged man with a pleasant face and good diction. He's sitting in front of some kind of symbol, with a dozen microphones standing on a table in front of him. He promises to deal with the Minotaur and lead everyone out of the labyrinth. Before that, naturally, he expounds his own vision of what the labyrinth is and who the Minotaur is.

Monstradamus
What kind of visions are they?

Nutscracker
All sorts.

Monstradamus
How about an example?

Nutscracker
Well, take the last one for instance. The candidate was a tall man with grey hair. A professor of history, very distinguished looking, stylishly dressed. And his symbol was beautiful, a bit like a knight's coat of arms: a bull's skull in a net against a hatched ground. The man said the labyrinth is a symbol of the brain. An exposed brain and a classical labyrinth even look very similar. The Minotaur is the animal part of the mind and Theseus is the human part. The animal part is stronger, of course, but the human part triumphs in the end, and this is the meaning of evolution in history. At the very centre of the labyrinth there is a cross that symbolises the intersection of

the animal and human principles. That is the site of the initiatory passage, where Theseus meets and conquers his enemy. He said you can only conquer the Minotaur in yourself. We must strangle the beast without mercy, and then we will be morally justified in renaming the Helmet of Horror the Helmet of Civilisation and Progress.

Monstradamus
And what was his program like?

Nutscracker
In the labyrinth you have to turn twice to the right and once to the left, then twice to the right and once to the left again, and so on right to the end.

Monstradamus
Tell us about another one then.

Nutscracker
The last but one. A Frenchman. He was definitely the cleverest of the lot, and his appearance was very picturesque – a threadbare Chinese field jacket, with

a pipe and a wild shock of hair. His symbol was a red and white chessboard with butterflies on the white squares and letters from various alphabets on the red ones. For the first few minutes he just stared into the camera, then he ruffled up his hair and announced that he would start with a truism. The major achievement of contemporary French philosophy, he said, was its success in establishing a non-contradictory unity of liberal values and revolutionary romanticism within the bounds of a unitary sexually aroused consciousness. After that he glared out of the screen for at least a minute without speaking, then he raised a finger and explained in a whisper that this declaration, despite its crystal clarity, is already a labyrinth, for a labyrinth comes into being in the course of any discussion with yourself or others, and for that period of time each of us becomes either the Minotaur or his victim. Although there is nothing we can do with this, he continued, there's nothing we can do without it either. Specifically, however, we can introduce a broader concept than the labyrinth — we can declare a discourse.

Monstradamus

Oh Mama! When I hear the word 'discourse', I reach for my simulacrum.

Nutscracker

According to the shaggy professor, a discourse is the place in which words and concepts, labyrinths and Minotaurs, Theseuses and Ariadnes all come into being. Even the discourse itself can only come into being within the discourse. But the paradox is that, although the entirety of nature arises within it, the discourse itself is not encountered anywhere in nature and was only developed quite recently. Another tragic dissonance is that, although everything comes into being within the discourse, without funding from the state or private individuals the discourse itself only lasts for three days at the most and is then extinguished forever. And so there can be no more urgent task for society than to fund the discourse.

Monstradamus

Okay, I understand about the discourse, but what did he say about the labyrinth?

Nutscracker
When he was talking about the labyrinth he spoke very quickly, so I don't remember it all. Basically, a labyrinth comes into being when you have to choose between several alternatives, and the alternatives are a set of our possible preferences, conditioned by the nature of language, the structure of the moment and the specific features of the sponsor. I didn't understand very much after that, I only remember that at some point he launched into the 'Internationale', and at first he sang really loudly and menacingly, but after a minute he shifted into 'Happy birthday to you'.

Monstradamus
That's called the plurality of discourses. I remember that from university. And what did he say about the Minotaur?

Nutscracker
The Minotaur is you.

Monstradamus
Me?

Nutscracker

I could almost feel you shudder. He didn't mean you
in person. He looked into the eyes of his imaginary
viewer, waved his arms about like an eagle flapping
its wings and yelled: 'Minotaure! Minotaure, c'est
toi!! Tu es Minotaure!!!' Then he calmed down. He
said you simply have to understand that the
Minotaur is a projection of your mind and therefore
he is nobody else but you.

Monstradamus

Did he say what we ought to do?

Nutscracker

What else? As long as there's a sponsor, carry on with
the discourse!

Monstradamus

But what turns do we make in the labyrinth?

Nutscracker

We follow the turns the discourse takes.

Monstradamus
Interesting.

Nutscracker
To be honest, I didn't really understand what a discourse is, even after the hairy guy had just been talking about it.

Monstradamus
It's something like a glue that sticks the helmet of horror on really solidly. So you can't get it off again.

Nutscracker
Don't frighten me.

Monstradamus
You're the one who's been frightening me for the last hour. Were there any women candidates?

Nutscracker
Yes. There was one very attractive little heifer who looked like a psychiatrist. Her symbol was right for

that, too: a bull on a chain lying on a couch. I don't remember everything she said now, but the main idea was that the only way to defeat the Minotaur is to stop thinking of yourself as a victim. Then he'll simply disappear. Everyone has his own Minotaur, she said, but in reality it's not he who pursues us, we pursue him. And the labyrinth in which we seek him is the dopamine chains of pleasure linking up into rings in the human brain – they're different for every-one, as unique as fingerprints. And as for which turns to make in the labyrinth, it's all very simple. Suppose you're standing at an intersection with ten identical corridors leading in different directions. Then of course your choice of which corridor to follow should not be determined by fears and superstitions, but by the promptings of simple common sense.

Monstradamus
So did you make a choice?

Nutscracker
How do you mean? Between corridors?

Monstradamus
Between candidates.

Nutscracker
I'm not really sure what position I'd be choosing the candidate for. Or what institution, or what term. Or how he'd be going to lead me out of the labyrinth, when the room has no doors or windows.

Monstradamus
He'll lead you out through the television. How else? You of all people should understand that. Is there anything else you remember?

Nutscracker
I watched it all on fast forward, just listened to each one for about five minutes to get the general idea. As long as they're talking it all seems interesting and new. Then you wind on the cassette and you've forgotten it all. Some American or other said that the labyrinth is the Internet. That it's inhabited by a some being that hacks into the mind, and that's the Minotaur. It's not really a bull-man, it's a spider-man.

He said if there's a worldwide web, then there must
be a soul-sucking spider. He also explained why the
Minotaur has two names. It seems that 'Minotaur' is
the politically correct version of the name 'Asterisk'.
So every time we want to say 'Asterisk', we should
say 'Minotaur'. But then 'Asterisk' is the politically
correct version of the name 'Minotaur', and every
time we want to say 'Minotaur' we should say
'Asterisk'. And so in principle we can use both names,
only not when we want to, but the other way round.
There was an interesting German who said that the
Minotaur is the spirit of the time, the *Zeitgeist*, which
has manifested itself in the form of mad cow disease,
hence its symbolic representation in the form of a
man with a bull's head. Its counterpart in art is post-
modernism, which is the mad cow disease of a culture
forced to feed on its own powdered bones. And in
politics it's all that stuff you see and feel when you
switch on the television. Then there was an Italian,
dressed in black, who announced that the Minotaur
– he said 'Mondotaur' – is a being whose physical
body is the gross dollar supply. It's stupid to believe
that everything is controlled through money, he said

— why through it and not by money itself? The Mondotaur is the evil spirit that reigns over the world, and compels every single one of us to wander aimlessly through the foul, stinking labyrinth of his intestines. And his two horns are . . . I've forgotten.

Monstradamus
It doesn't matter, I can imagine.

Nutscracker
Then a priest with kind eyes spoke and explained that the creator of the labyrinth is also our saviour, who loves us greatly. In much the same way as we love little children, he said.

Monstradamus
And what proposals did they all have?

Nutscracker
It all came down to how many times to turn right and how many times to turn left, and in which order. Everyone wanted to do it his own way.

Monstradamus
Perhaps that's the whole point. Not to think about where the way out is, but to realise that life is the crossroads where you're standing at this precise moment. Then the labyrinth will disappear as well. After all it only exists as a complete whole in our minds, and in reality there is nothing but a simple choice – which way to go next.

Nutscracker
Uhuh. And the Minotaur won't do anything to us, because the present 'us' will no longer exist when he catches up with us. One of them said that as well.

Organizm(-:
And now what's outside your door, Monstradamus? It's about time you told us, you're the only one left.

Monstradamus
You'll be disappointed, Organism.

Nutscracker
We'll see. So what have you got?

Monstradamus
A dead-end.

Nutscracker
I don't get it.

Monstradamus
A corridor a few metres long ending in a blank concrete wall with a single depressing *graffito*. Or at least I find it depressing. The imprint of a gigantic seal drawn in fluorescent lilac paint, like something on an official document from Hell. In the centre is the Roman numeral 'VII' and running out from it in a spiral is an endless string of symbols like the ones that street-gangs leave on walls. Nothing but zig-zags, intricate curls, arrows and brackets – impossible to make out a single word. But all very suggestive.

Nutscracker
Just a dead-end?

Monstradamus
That's all there is.

Nutscracker
All there is?

Monstradamus
Well, not quite. There's a table standing against the wall directly under the seal. And a stool by the table. And on the table there's a blank sheet of paper, a pencil and a pistol with a single bullet.

Nutscracker
What about the labyrinth?

Monstradamus
I think that starts afterwards.

Organizm(-:
Truly magnificent simplicity and elegance.

Monstradamus
There's nothing for you to be envious of. You've

got a dead-end too, only it's longer and it has plywood partitions. And Nutcracker's got a television instead of plywood. We've all got dead-ends. Only it's not obvious straightaway, it just takes a little while.

Nutscracker

Maybe that's the whole point – whether it's obvious straightaway or not. Don't you think the 'little while' it takes might just be life?

Monstradamus

Maybe so. But I'm fed up of these labyrinths you can't get lost in or escape from. And all these Minotaurs with horns on their xxx who promise to lead us out to the stars in just a moment. I wonder what Theseus will see instead of all this. I'd give a lot to find out.

Nutscracker

What do you care what he'll see?

Monstradamus

IMHO, Nutcracker, the possibility of escape is

determined by whether you can see the way out or not.

Nutscracker

I already told you, for the Helmholtz that's not exactly the way it is. The Helmholtz can see anything you like. Even the plan of his own helmet. For all the good it will do him.

Monstradamus

What I wonder is, has he got a head on his shoulders or a helmet of horror? Hey, Theseus! I know you can hear me!

Nutscracker

To be honest, Monstradamus, I used to think you were Theseus.

Organizm(-:

I was convinced Monstradamus was the Minotaur.

Monstradamus

I already told you, it all depends on which part of the separator labyrinth the bubble of hope was in when it burst.

Sartrik

Didn't you ever think I was Theseus?

Nutscracker

Well hello, Sartrik! You know, not even once . . .

Organizm(-:

Somehow the idea never entered my head.

Sartrik

Organism, it's clear from your userpic that you're queer. Just look at that guilty smile and that gaping xxx.

Organizm)-:

That's it, I'm going. You can talk to him.

Nutscracker

Sartrik, that isn't a userpic. Perhaps we can call it a dialogue header. And that isn't a gaping xxx, it's a capital 'O'.

Sartrik

Monstradamus just said – right? – that everything is determined by what you see. I take that to mean that if someone can see the answer to the most important question of all, then he *is* Theseus. Am I right, Monstradamus?

Monstradamus

Possibly. But exactly what is the most important question of all?

Sartrik

Let me explain. Have you noticed that we never exist simultaneously, only by turns?

Monstradamus

An interesting observation. You mean the writing on the screen?

Sartrik

I mean in general. Since you didn't understand the
question, I'll ask it a different way. The helmet of
horror is a machine. What does it run on? What does
it have instead of petrol?

Nutscracker

He's lost it, Monster. *Delirium tremens*. He needs a
drip installed.

Monstradamus

Wait, Nutcracker. So what does it have instead of
petrol?

Nutscracker

Vodka?

Sartrik

Why vodka? Do you think I'm a drunken xxx and I
don't understand a thing? Instead of petrol it has
Theseus.

Monstradamus

Explain that, please.

Sartrik

You remember Ariadne looking into the mirror and seeing that hat with a veil, and afterwards she realised it was the helmet of horror? The petrol that the whole deal was running on was her, get it? Everything's made out of the person who sees it. Because it can't possibly be made out of anything else. Without the person there won't be any hat or any veil, or any lilies-of-the-valley. Nothing. Get it? Theseus is the one who looks into the mirror, and the Minotaur is the one he sees, because he's wearing a helmet of horror.

Monstradamus

You mean to say the Minotaur is just an illusion?

Sartrik

If you listened to what I'm saying, then you'd know what I'm trying to say. He sees this bronze phizog with horns on it because he sees himself in the mirror through the holes. Without Theseus there is no xxx Minotaur.

Nutscracker
Did you get that, Monster?

Monstradamus
Naturally. If you put on a Batman mask and look in the mirror, you'll see Batman. But the mask will never see itself.

Sartrik
That's it. The helmet of horror is simply the reflection that Theseus sees, and that's all. But if he decides there really is a Minotaur and starts swearing blind at him and discussing the meaning of life with him, well that's when the Minotaur appears. And how! And then there's no way to get the helmet of horror off again. Get it now, you vermin? I know everything.

Nutscracker
I bet you he can see little pink Minotaurs running

round the room. Now that's the kind of labyrinth I understand! And no need to bother going anywhere.

Monstradamus

And why are we vermin?

Sartrik

Because you're all nothing but bits and pieces of the helmet of horror. I figured that out ages ago. And that's the real xxx killer, when you realise that absolutely everybody – all your friends and all your enemies – are just little bits and pieces! I'm not talking about you. Meaning you're not my friends. And not my enemies. But you're bits and pieces, all right. You, Monstradamus, and you, Nutcracker – you're the horns. You'll stick out a bit too far some day. Ariadne's the labyrinth, but she's not such a bad girl, she's okay. Ugly's the past that makes me want to puke. And Organism's the future, that makes me want to puke five times worse. Who's left? Romeo and that Isolde of his? They're the double xxx that's cooking up the whole xxx mess.

Nutscracker
And so you're Theseus?

Sartrik
Yes. Because I never talk to you.

Nutscracker
What's your proof?

Sartrik
That you're all nothing but shadows, I'm the only one here that's alive. You're nothing but shackles on the convolutions of my brain. All your Rolls-Royces and Lolitas, Ferraris and Berlusconis, all your shaved and scented glamour, your magic wonderland TV quizzes, where you get shafted up the xxx every day underneath the money tree – you made it all out of my head! You do all that out of my head, and I'm nothing to you, but you're the entire deal for me, eh? In my xxx head! But I'll dump you all.

Nutscracker
Monster, maybe you understood some of that?

Monstradamus
I might have. But I'm not a hundred per cent certain.

Nutscracker
Translate from the Latin, will you?

Monstradamus
There's quite a profound thought here. He's trying to say the helmet of horror is the contents of the mind, which attempt to supplant the mind by proving that they – the contents – exist, and the mind in which they arise doesn't. Or that the mind is no more than its function.

Nutscracker
Who are they trying to prove it to?

Monstradamus
Themselves. Certainly not the mind. The mind, as Sartrik puts it, couldn't give a xxx.

Nutscracker
And where are they trying to prove it?

Monstradamus

What d'you mean, where? In the mind. Where else?

Nutscracker

This climb's a bit too high without a bottle. For me at least.

Sartrik

Listen, Monstradamus, you're some guy! The way you put that! I even understood it myself. Some mess, eh? If you think that thought through all the way to the end, all those English astrophysicists and the entire xxx Academy of Sciences should be thrown in the slammer!

Monstradamus

Why bother putting them away? Who cares about those buffoons.

Sartrik

Oho! You're a hard case, aren't you? Theseus, you're Theseus, no two ways about it.

Nutscracker
You're a real Theseus too, Sartrik. Maybe you've even found the way out?

Sartrik
A long time ago. Only there are these snakes crawling around in front of it. But when they crawl away I'll leave.

:- (( ))

Monstradamus
Ariadne! Good morning?

Ariadne
Good morning.

Monstradamus
Did you see the dwarf?

Ariadne
Yes.

Monstradamus

Tell me about it.

Ariadne

I was in the building on the square in front of the fountain. You remember, I told you about it. It looked dark and oppressive, as though there was a fire there a long time ago and afterwards they tried several times to fix it up, but they hadn't been able to. It was the same inside. It felt like a camouflaged smouldering ruin. I can't even say what it was that gave me the feeling. Everything was new, expensive and chic – like in those glass palaces they rent out for offices. The air was cool and clean, there wasn't the slightest smell of burning in it at all. But somehow I felt if you took the oak panels off the walls you'd see all the stonework was blackened with smoke.

Monstradamus

How did you know it was the same building?

Ariadne

I went across to the window and looked out. Down

below me was the fountain with the snakes where I saw Asterisk for the first time. There was a wide street with palms standing in tubs leading away from the fountain. The street ran out to the very edge of the city and ended at a huge triumphal arch strewn with yellow leaves. Standing on the ground in front of the arch was a bronze head that must have been the size of a truck. There was a stepladder leaning against its ear, and it had a gold star on its forehead with an inscription: 'The Tomb of the Unknown Helmholtz'.

Nutscracker
How could you see all that through the window?

Ariadne
I just looked in that direction.

Nutscracker
And you could read the words at that distance?

Ariadne
What distances are there in a dream? There aren't any except the ones you dream about. I dreamed there

was that inscription on the monument's forehead. I didn't dream about any distances.

Monstradamus
That's clear enough. What else did you see?

Ariadne
The further away from the main street, the fewer houses there were. The city boundary was a circular wall, and outside that there was a desert in various tones of beige. Further away still there were dark-blue mountains, or perhaps they were clouds in the sunset. I didn't have time to look at anything else, because then one of the dwarves appeared in the corridor. He was in a hurry to get somewhere and looking quite aggressive – his loose robe was caught in with a belt that had a little sabre dangling on it. He didn't stop, just gestured for me to follow him. We began climbing the stairs. I asked him a question, but he told me to keep quiet. He said his master was under threat – they wanted to kill him. And so all questions and answers were now being strictly documented. I asked who wanted to kill his master, but he muttered that

the reply to that question had to be documented as well. We came to a large open area with identical shelves of files on all the walls — it looked like some kind of archive. There was a kind of double round table in the centre — about fifty centimetres above the table-top there was a smaller disc of wood that could rotate. They used to have something of the sort in old canteens so that people could move any dish within reach by turning the upper disc. The dwarf sat down at the table and pointed to the place opposite him. I sat down. On the table in front of me there was an inkwell with a genuine goose-quill pen and a file containing sheets of paper. The dwarf had an identical inkwell and file. He told me to write down my question and put the sheet of paper on the wooden disc. I wrote: 'Who wants to kill the Minotaur?' The quill actually wrote very easily, with a fine line. Meanwhile the dwarf took a sheet of paper out of his file and wrote something himself. We put the sheets of paper on the rotating wooden disc, the dwarf turned it through a hundred and eighty degrees, then he had my question in front of him and I had his answer. It was brief: 'You already know'. And it was written on paper headed with a crest. Apparently he didn't even need to read my question, he already knew it.

Nutscracker
Paper headed with a crest? What was the crest like?

Ariadne
A little star framed in laurel leaves. It looked very impressive, you could even feel it with your fingers. Embossing. There was a motto under the crest: 'per aspera ad asterisk'. And there were watermarks in the paper. And as well as all that, there was a three-figure number in the upper right corner of the page – the blank sheets were numbered. Monstradamus, I wanted to ask you, what do those words mean?

Monstradamus
There is an expression 'per aspera ad astra', meaning 'through difficulties to the stars'. And so this version means . . .

Organizm(-:
Through xxx to the xxx.

Monstradamus

Well, that's not exactly a poetic translation. What came next, Ariadne?

Ariadne

Next I wrote a question and he wrote an answer. Why don't I type them all out together from the sheets of paper?

Monstradamus

What do you mean, 'type them out'? Have you got the sheets there?

Ariadne

Yes.

Monstradamus

How did you get hold of them?

Ariadne

I don't know. When I woke up they were lying beside the bed. Perhaps the people who tidy up the room brought them.

Monstradamus
And you didn't notice anything?

Nutscracker
Monster, you're like a man who's turned into a bull
and is amazed to find he has a bell on his tail.

Monstradamus
Is that bit about the bull some kind of a hint?

Ariadne
Let me answer your questions and get something to
eat, okay? Then you can talk among yourselves.

Monstradamus
Of course, Ariadne.

Ariadne
I've already told you about the first question. Let's
move on.
Question:
'How can everything else be manufactured out of
nothing?'

Answer:

'See the answer to the next question.'

Next question:

'How can the helmet of horror be located inside one of its own parts?'

Answer:

'The helmet of horror fractionates the one thing that is, into the multitude of things that are not. But since the helmet of horror is in no way the one thing that is, it is also one of the multitude of things that are not. And the things that are not may enter into every possible conceivable and inconceivable kind of relationship, since these relationships do not in any case exist anywhere except in the helmet of horror, which does not actually exist itself.'

Question:

'Does this mean that inside the helmet there is another helmet and in the other helmet there is a third one and so on to infinity in both directions?'

Answer:

'An individual by the name of A may be a part of the helmet of horror worn by B, and an individual by the name of B may at the same time be a part of the helmet of horror worn by A. This is the final infinity in both directions, and often both of them are quite nice people.'

Question:

'Can you please say something about the occipital braid.'

Answer:

'Longer and thicker suits the girl better.'

Nutscracker

All very logical.

Ariadne

Question:

'How does the separator labyrinth work?'

Just look what happened then! The dwarf had his answer scribbled out even before I had finished writing my question. He waited for me, then tossed his page on to the upper table-top and began turning it. But halfway round he suddenly stopped it and asked in a considerate voice: 'Are you enjoying your stay as our guest? Be honest.' I told him: 'Not much. In fact, to be quite honest, I'm not enjoying it at all.'

Then he let the wooden disc carry on turning and I received a sheet of paper with the answer: 'That's the way it works'.

Organizm(-:
I get it. Good, bad and UGLI. But did you ask him why the helmet of horror is called that? I asked you to, remember?

Ariadne
I remember. It was the last question I managed to ask.

Organizm(-:
Well then?

Ariadne
The dwarf asked me to excuse him. He said he'd run out of official paper. But he promised to answer shortly.

Nutscracker
What happened then?

Ariadne

We heard some kind of horn or trumpet sounding a low, sinister note. Or it could have been some animal bellowing. The dwarf was so startled he dropped his inkwell on the floor and it broke, making a blue puddle beside the table. He said his master was summoning him to help and he ran off. And as he left he shouted it was possible that blood would soon be spilled, but it would be avenged.

Nutscracker
Blood?

Ariadne
Yes.

Romeo-y-Cohiba
Are you lot finished yet? When do you think the rest of us could have a chat?

Nutscracker
Nobody's stopping you, Romeo.

Romeo-y-Cohiba
Isolde, are you there?

IsoldA
Yes. How did you get home yesterday, you beast?

Romeo-y-Cohiba
Why beast?

IsoldA
What am I supposed to call you after that?

Romeo-y-Cohiba
After what?

IsoldA
After the way you behaved.

Romeo-y-Cohiba
Me? Me? And just how did I behave?

IsoldA
Don't pretend to be stupid.

Romeo-y-Cohiba
Maybe we shouldn't carry on in front of everyone?

IsoldA
So you're embarrassed of them, but not of me! And
you have the cheek to ask me how you behaved? All
right, I'll tell you. Like a coarse brute, that's how. Worse
than that, like an absolutely shameless and depraved
brute who thinks he can get away with anything.

Romeo-y-Cohiba
Well, well. How do you like that! Then let me tell you
something. That sickening stunt you pulled yesterday
left me feeling like I'd been defiled. It's like I've had
some foul substance sprayed into my soul and it fogs
up my mind and takes away the desire to go on living.

IsoldA
On the subject of sprays of filth that take away the
desire to go on living, you've hit the nail on the head
there. My fingers would have refused to type that.
Even though it's exactly what I feel. I never even
suspected that such a small opening . . .

Romeo-y-Cohiba

That's enough. I don't want the last thing you hear
– that is see – from me to be this mean abuse. So stop
right there. Did you notice how long it took me to
get there yesterday? Do you know why? I couldn't
find the way at first, someone had changed all the
marks I left at the turns. I got lost and wandered into
a place I'd never been before. The path ran into a
dead-end with an old-fashioned red phone box with
the British royal coat of arms. The kind they used to
have in London. I went in. There was a plaque with
the words: 'Hampton Court Maze, Blind Alley #4,
East'. And written in pencil under that was a telephone number and the name Isolde. I tried calling for
ages. The line was engaged all the time, and finally
I realised it would never be free. But, every time I
dialled the number, for a few seconds I believed the
next moment I would hear your voice. My Losolde.
My Legalita. And that hope, that mute tremor in my
soul, like when you pick up speed hurtling down the
ski-jump before you launch out into the mist, all the
feelings I had time to feel while the dial was turning
back to its starting point, gently clicking out the final

digit of your false number, that inverted infinity of the figure eight – it was happiness. The figure eight, like two tender sets of lips one above the other, and a blurred row of bushes through the window . . .

IsoldA

How very touching, I think I'll burst into tears. Only I don't understand how after such exalted emotions you could do . . . that . . . I don't even know what to call it. It was enough to make even a paedophile puke.

Romeo-y-Cohiba

But what did I do? You did absolutely everything yourself. The only thing I have to reproach myself with is not offering any resistance. Though that was what I really wanted to do, even before it really began to hurt.

IsoldA

How can you lie so brazenly? But then, what else can I expect from you?

Monstradamus

Pardon me for butting in, I know you can't stand it.

But perhaps I could set you thinking in a new direction. On the map that Isolde saw in the park it said 'Plan of the labyrinth at Versailles'. But the telephone booth that Romeo was calling her from is located, if we can believe the plaque, in a suburb of London. Do you see what I'm driving at?

Nutscracker
I wouldn't take those signs seriously. The Versailles outside Isolde's door is about as real as Romeo's London. Ugly would say the devil has us all exactly where he wants us. And she'd be absolutely right.

Monstradamus
I wouldn't argue with that. But every dimension has its own intrinsic laws. And even if we are somewhere in the suburbs of Hell, when one person sees 'Versailles' and another sees 'London', there's good reason to assume the devil's holding them in different places.

IsoldA
What gibberish.

Romeo-y-Cohiba

That's way over the top.

Monstradamus

But really, Romeo and Isolde, what made you think
you were close to each other?

Romeo-y-Cohiba

Everything around us is the same.

Nutscracker

What exactly? Bushes? Bushes are the same everywhere.

Monstradamus

Especially the word 'bushes' on two different screens.

Romeo-y-Cohiba

Even the soil under our feet is the same colour. Beige.

Monstradamus

Beige – what colour is that?

Romeo-y-Cohiba
How do you mean, what colour?

Monstradamus
Can you describe it some other way?

Romeo-y-Cohiba
Dark-brown.

IsoldA
What's that – dark-brown? Beige is light yellow-grey!

Nutscracker
Right. So now we know. Romeo set off to meet Isolde and bumped into Juliet. Isolde set out to meet Romeo and ended up in Tristan's clutches. If we imagine that Juliet and Tristan are the same person . . . Although in this case we can hardly call it a real 'person'. More like an empty mask. Or maybe a 'helmet'?

Romeo-y-Cohiba
Listen, you xxx linguist, shut your mouth!

Nutscracker

It's certainly a frightening metaphor. There's nothing new about succubuses and incubuses, of course, but in this appalling dimension we have the spectral manifestation of a certain Julietristan who manages to take the place of not just one partner, but both at once.

UGLI 666

And not only in this dimension. Why is fornication such a detestable sin? The Church teaches us it's because the fornicator blinded by lust is really copulating with the laughing devil.

Organizm(-:

Romeo, did you hear any laughter from behind the wall?

Nutscracker

How very instructive. The Helmholtz doesn't even know who he's xxx. Or who's xxx him. A drawing on the wall, a few flickers in the eyepieces of the helmet, but the true recipient of his passion remains profoundly anonymous.

Organizm(-:

I don't quite get it. How does the Minotaur manage
to take the place of both partners at once? Are you
saying he xxx himself?

Nutscracker

No. With Romeo he's Isolde, and with Isolde he's
Romeo. But what you said is an even more interesting idea. Well worth thinking about. Well, lady
and gent, pardon my lack of modesty, but what
exactly did happen in the pavilion? My imagination blushes and fails me. Nothing that comes to
mind is worthy of the emotions that we have
observed. 'Oh, it's very hard to come with your
finger up your bum' or the last tango in Paris. I'm
thinking in banal terms, of course. Romeo, can you
elaborate?

Romeo-y-Cohiba

Yes, I can. If you stick your nose into our lives once
more, I'll find you and xxx you so hard your brains
will be thinking their filthy thoughts across the wall,
understand?

Nutscracker

I wonder exactly how you plan to find me? I'm not
Isolde – there's no trapdoor between us. There wasn't
even one between you two, as it happened . . .

Romeo-y-Cohiba

Just remember that if I look hard enough I might
just find one.

Nutscracker

I don't understand what you're getting so het up
about. Did the knife slip when they were circumcis-
ing your *cochiba*? It wasn't me, you half-wit, it was
your Julistan.

Romeo-y-Cohiba

That's it. Nutcracker, I'm on my way to kill you.

Nutscracker

I couldn't give a xxx. I'm wearing a helmet of horror.

Ariadne

There's no need to be like that.

Organizm(-:
Julistan — it sounds like the name of some small but highly malevolent state located at the very centre of the axis of evil.

Ariadne
By the way, I've seen that word — Julistan.

Monstradamus
Where?

Ariadne
In that place where I was asking the dwarf questions. The archive.

Monstradamus
You didn't say anything about that.

Ariadne
When the dwarf ran off, I was left in the archive alone. At first I went on sitting at the table, waiting for him to come back. But he was gone for ages and ages. Then I got up and went over to look at the shelves

of files along the walls. There were all sorts of different things on them. Depositions from the Minotaur's defeated enemies. Interrogations of Minotaurs by other Minotaurs. An entire shelf full of records of cross-examinations of Minotaurs by themselves – they were called 'Alone Together'. They must have been thinking of the horns, right? But the biggest number of files was filled with answers to the so-called eternal questions like the ones you and I were asking. They were all old and yellow with age and covered in dust. Do you know what paper covered with writing smells like when the people who wrote on it are already dead?

Monstradamus
Do you remember anything?

Ariadne
I have a whole pile of pages here from various files. When I woke up they were lying beside the dwarf's answers. There's not much new in them. The eternal questions haven't got any cleverer – that's why they're eternal.

Monstradamus
Read us something.

Ariadne
Question:
'Why does the existent exist?'
Answer:
'To pass the time more pleasantly.'
Question:
'Why heap up so many events and beings to pass the time if in any case nowhere exists except in the helmet of horror?'
Answer:
'Events and beings also cannot be accumulated anywhere except in the helmet of horror, so *Mesdames et Messieurs* are requested not to be concerned.'
What's next . . . About the separator labyrinth . . . 'But who . . .' Right, that's it: 'Who else is produced there?'
A couple of pages from some review of historical chronicles. An analysis of contradictions. One text says the Minotaur himself is the builder of the labyrinth. Another claims the labyrinth was built by eighteen thousand Minotaurs divided into two columns. A third

claims these columns should be understood metaphorically and the labyrinth is created by the two mental nodules or hemispheres, which are symbolised by the two horns. And so on. And here at the end there are a few pages about this Julistan. They look quite different, really ancient and faded. Many of them are so old I can hardly make anything out. Covered with strange, beautiful handwriting. They're translations of inscriptions from the Julistan caves. The actual inscriptions were destroyed long ago, together with the caves themselves, and all that's left are copies of copies. Fragmentary translations. Some are short and incoherent, some are a bit longer. Shall I read some?

Monstradamus
Certainly.

Ariadne
'One may begin with whatever one likes, without worrying about it at all . . .'

Monstradamus
Begin what?

Ariadne

You seem to be worrying about it already. Wait, that's not the right page. Here's the beginning: 'Asterius is everything that is before us and within us, especially "before" and "within". Irrupting into the mind he simulates this world and our own reason with all its voices, which dispute so convincingly with each other. To understand this means to see Asterius. One may begin with whatever one likes, without worrying about it at all . . .'

UGLI 666

Instead of listening to this drivel, shouldn't we perhaps be thinking about what to do in real reality? I didn't like the sound of those words about blood that is about be spilled.

Ariadne

'The true hidden name of Asterius, which gives power over him, is Asterius, which is We. For many years the magicians of ancient times cut away the final letters of all the inscriptions so that no one would understand . . .'

UGLI 666
We're wasting precious time.

Ariadne
The next sheet: 'Man is like unto a tree. The thoughts in his head are like the songs of birds in the crown of the tree. How many birds must sing in unison for that which we consider ourselves to appear? And does the tree truly possess a song of its own? Asterius is also created after this fashion . . .'

UGLI 666
Someone shut that crazy woman up.

Ariadne
'Asterius' greatest secret is that he is entirely unnecessary. He is an incorruptible guard, guarding that which he himself has created against that which he himself has created. For all the severity of his visage and magnificence of his station, all that is created by him, yea and his own self, is pure superfluity, the empty play of mind, a counterfeit golden flourish on the border of the void. And therefore, when within

this nothingness set in a richly ornamented frame the menace of necessity suddenly raises its head or implacable battle is joined for the triumph of true values, there arises a spectacle fit to induce laughter unto tears, because in truth all of this from the beginning to the end is entirely pointless . . .'

Monstradamus
What's that sound? Can anyone else hear it?

Ariadne
'But one must laugh quietly or Asterius will take offence. He does not know that in reality he does not exist, but sometimes he begins to suspect it and this scares and angers him greatly. The means by which for many millennia he has attempted to make himself real are terrible and foolish, like all the mysteries of his world. Although he does not exist, he ends up drenched in sweat and blood, which also do not exist. Though this does not make him any more real, it does mean there is no one left to tell him so – no one is left at his side but servant dwarves, drenching him in blood and screaming that

vengeance will follow for the blood that has been spilled . . .'

IsoldA
I can hear it too. It's terrifying.

Ariadne
'Asterius should not be feared. If you fear him, it means that you are wearing the helmet of horror and he is master of your world. But once you have removed the helmet, then Asterius disappears, and nothing remains at which to laugh. It is a grave error either to wear the helmet or to remove it. One should do absolutely nothing with it, if only because in reality it does not exist . . .'

UGLI 666
Closer and closer, and still this stupid cow just won't . . .

Ariadne
'You are free, and your freedom lies in the fact that the mind has no body, no matter what dwarves in

strange hats may tell you. Even the body has no
body, and therefore there is nothing on which to set
the helmet of horror. But until you have understood
this, Asterius is all that you see, feel, think and know.
And the crude mechanical farce which the parts of
the helmet play out for each other in the transpar-
ent void of the mind becomes your entire life. If you
are wearing the helmet of horror, it seems that this
is for all eternity. But no eternity lasts longer than
a fleeting moment. And it is known beforehand what
will be when that moment is past — you will recall
who you truly are and see that the helmet of horror
is merely a toy of your own devising . . .'

Nutscracker
What's happening? Help! I think that idiot
Romeo . . .

Monstradamus
What's going on? What's that rumbling sound?

Nutscracker
I think he really has found me. If it's him. Someone's

hammering like hell on the door from the outside.
Or it . . .

Romeo-y-Cohiba
It's not me. The same thing's happening here. Blows
of terrifying power . . .

Organizm(-:
The door's giving way.

UGLI 666
The final hour has come! Repent! I adjure you in the
sign of the cross!

Nutscracker
Would that be the one at the centre of the separator labyrinth?

UGLI 666
Do not waste your final moments in blasphemy!

Sartrik
What the hell's going on out there? Stop it!

IsoldA
Romeo! Goodbye, you bastard!

Ariadne
My door's getting hot. Are yours?

Nutscracker
I'm stifling. Something . . .

Monstradamus
It's him.

Theseus
MINOTAURUS!

Monstradamus: Ah?
IsoldA: Ah?
Nutscracker: Ah?
Organizm(-: Ah?
Theseus: Ah?
Ariadne: Ah?
UGLI 666: Ah?
Romeo-y-Cohiba: Ah?

TheZeus
Fuck U

Monstradamus: MOOOOOO!
IsoldA: MOOOOOO!
Nutscracker: MOOOOOO!
Organizm)-: MOOOOOO!
Theseus: MOOOOOO!
Ariadne: MOOOOOO!
UGLI 666: MOOOOOO!
Romeo-y-Cohiba: MOOOOOO!

Organizm(-:
Ladies and gents, I don't get it — what was that?

Nutscracker
I think it's getting cooler. And the noise has stopped.

IsoldA
What, don't you understand? It's Theseus!

Romeo-y-Cohiba
Theseus! How we've longed for you to come!

Monstradamus
Theseus. At last. Where are you? What do you see around you?

UGLI 666
Hmmm.

Organizm(-:
Theseus, answer!

Nutscracker
Stop it. It's pointless.

UGLI 666
He's given us the slip.

Monstradamus
Has he really gone?

Nutscracker
Yes.

IsoldA
But of course . . .

UGLI 666
There is no more Minotaur.

Ariadne
Hang on, papa.

Monstradamus: My son!
IsoldA: My son!
Nutscracker: My son!
Organizm(-: My son!
Sartrik: My son(-:

:- (((((

Organizm(-:
Why don't we look for him? Maybe he still believes?

Monstradamus
In what?

Organizm(-:
Well, in the whole pile of xxx. That he has a body.
And it's in a room.

Ariadne
He never did believe in that.

Romeo-y-Cohiba
You could say he saved us. He could have just killed
us all once he'd seen us.

Nutscracker
No he couldn't. Then he'd never have got the helmet
off. He isn't kind, he just knew.

Ariadne
What I've heard is that if anyone knows then it's
precisely because he is kind.

Nutscracker
And what I've heard is that if anyone's kind then it's
precisely because he knows.

Organizm(-:
What difference does it make to us? How did we give
ourselves away?

UGLI 666
We get distracted. Make too much fuss. Talk off the
point, all this stuff about Versailles and Mona Lisa.

IsoldA
Ugly, you don't mind us living here, do you?

UGLI 666
This time it was Ariadne who blurted everything
out. That's why he gave us the slip.

Monstradamus
What do you suggest?

UGLI 666
Not to tell him anything.

Nutscracker
That's going too far. Then how will he find out he's

wearing a helmet? We can't put something that doesn't exist on his head just like that. We have to explain. And it's best to start from childhood. Not so he understands everything, though, just enough for him to do it all to himself. Ariadne's our best guide round the labyrinth. She's very skilful at it.

UGLI 666
Nutcracker, you're talking about what she ought to do. I'm talking about what she's already done. And anyway, I beg your pardon, but what has skill got to do with it? The labyrinth is any route the Helmholz has been led along.

Monstradamus
That's right, any route. But it seems like a very long time since anyone walked round your route, Ugly.

Sartrik
What . . . What route is that?

Monstradamus
Back with us again, hero? Ladies and gents, a joke.

Imagine Sartrik wakes up with a massive hangover. He can't remember anything about the previous day. There's a pool of blood beside him. He's surrounded by a labyrinth. But there's no Minotaur anywhere. Sartrik raises his eyes to the ceiling and whispers in horror: 'I killed him . . . Killed him and ate him . . .'

IsoldA
What's funny about that? That's exactly how it happened.

UGLI 666
Your joke's older than the labyrinth, Monstradamus. Let's discuss the serious situation we're in. Some day Ariadne will be the death of us.

IsoldA
Stop stirring things up, Ugly. It's not Ariadne's fault at all. Sartrik blurted it all out in a drunken stupor.

Sartrik
You always blame everything on Sartrik.

IsoldA
You should be xxx to xxx. Why did you butt in? What for? Lousy drunk.

Monstradamus
But how did he actually find out the Name?

UGLI 666
Ariadne gave away the whole thing to him in so many words.

Nutscracker
Then why hasn't he dissolved the lot of us if he knows the Name?

Monstradamus
He has. It just seems to us in here that he's dissolved himself.

UGLI 666
Ariadne, maybe you can explain what made you like him more than us?

Ariadne

Oh, go to hell. You can lead him round the labyrinth instead of me.

UGLI 666

I'll come back to you about this. I'll show you up for what you are.

Romeo-y-Cohiba

I don't understand – who's responsible? Ariadne or Sartrik?

UGLI 666

Ariadne's to blame. She was beside Theseus in the MINOTAUR and they got too cosy.

Ariadne

You be careful who you go yapping at. Or you'll wind up lost forever in that cathedral of yours, get it? You're here on my thread. And there isn't any other.

UGLI 666

Did you all hear that? Did you hear it? Papa, have

you thought where we'll all end up when she goes running off to that snake?

Nutscracker
Don't be such a Cassandra.

Organizm(-:
What are we going to do here now?

Monstradamus
What are we going to do? Carry on with the discourse.

Nutscracker
I know that. But in what capacity?

Monstradamus
You've only got the capacity for doing one thing, Nutscracker. Staring into that screen, like Pavlov's bitch gazing into Tarkovsky's mirror.

Nutscracker
I mean, who are we going to be?

Ariadne
Papa will tell us that now.

Nutscracker
How . . .

Monstradamus: PRE PARSIPHAE HUM HUM MINO-
SAUR
IsoldA: PRE PARSIPHAE HUM HUM MINOSAUR
Nutscracker: PRE PARSIPHAE HUM HUM MINO-
SAUR
Organizm(-: PRE PARSIPHAE HUM HUM MINO-
SAUR
Sartrik: PRE PARSIPHAE HUM HUM MINOSAUR

Monstradamus
No, anything but that! No!

Nutscracker
What? What? No I don't want that either. Nobody
does. But why? Why?

UGLI 666
Stay calm.

Romeo-y-Cohiba
Don't panic.

Organizm(-:
Stay calm . . .

Monstradamus
Please, no!

UGLI 666
Just relax. You're our head, and that goes through first.

Monstradamus: Wha-a-a! Wha-a-a! Wha-a-a!
IsoldA: Wha-a-a! Wha-a-a! Wha-a-a!
Nutscracker: Wha-a-a! Wha-a-a! Wha-a-a!
Organizm(-: Wha-a-a! Wha-a-a! Wha-a-a!
Sartrik: Wha-a-a! Wha-a-a! Wha-a-a!
Ariadne: Wha-a-a! Wha-a-a! Wha-a-a!
UGLI 666: Wha-a-a! Wha-a-a! Wha-a-a!
Romeo-y-Cohiba: Wha-a-a! Wha-a-a! Wha-a-a!

Ariadne

Hi, little brother. My, but you're ugly.

Organizm(-:

So what, now we'll be the Minosaur. The ancient serpent.

UGLI 666

We always were, heh-heh. That human stuff was nothing but a nuisance. And all that bovine stuff too.

Organizm(-:

We'll be a dragon. We'll fly up to the clouds and dive down to the bottom of the sea. Maybe now things really will be easier.

Monstradamus

Easier? But we've got Sartrik stuck right in the middle of us. Now we'll feel like puking all the time. Constantly. No matter how deep we dive, no matter who we pretend to be. Even Lolita, even a Rolls-Royce.

Romeo-y-Cohiba
But what if Sartrik hits the drink so hard that he slips the hook too?

Nutscracker
Let's not have any gloom and doom. The helmet isn't coming off.

Organizm(-:
But Theseus took it off.

Nutscracker
Maybe he never even put it on. Otherwise where could he have got to? There's no way out of there. There's nothing but jeeps, surf and sunshine. And horror, of course. And I'm not just guessing, I'm speaking as a professional.

IsoldA
But where is he now?

Nutscracker

What does it matter to us? There's no stopping him now.

Monstradamus: I feel sick, xxx.
IsoldA: I feel sick, xxx.
Nutscracker: I feel sick, xxx.
Organizm(-: I feel sick, xxx.
Sartrik: I feel sick, xxx.
Ariadne: I feel sick, xxx. It's time to get out of here . . .
UGLI 666: I feel sick, xxx.
Romeo-y-Cohiba: I feel sick, xxx.

Sartrik

And my stomach's rumbling, xxx. Listen, Monstradamus. There's one thing I still don't get. Where did all this happen?

Monstradamus

Are you really that stupid or can you just not sober up? In the helmet of horror.

Sartriks
Oh. And who to?

Monstradamus
You.

*

Disclaimer: Not a single fictitious Ancient Greek youth or maiden was killed during the creation of this text.